Treasure Found

TREASURE FOUND

TIM GROSSI

PREFACE

TREASURE:

As a noun: something valuable (such as money, jewels, gold, or silver) that is hidden or kept in a safe place

As a verb: to hold or keep as precious[1]

PART ONE

CHAPTER ONE

Virgil Thorne walked out of the meeting hall shaking his head slightly. The KGC meeting had just dispersed and he knew what he had to do. He gave Zack Washington a look and Zack knew exactly what it meant. Zack went out and retrieved the buggy for them to travel back to North Carolina.

It was 1858 and the Knights of the Golden Circle were meeting throughout the country, to enact the next phase of their plans. Virgil, representing his father, was a member of the financial end of the KGC in Richmond, VA. The political members were making policy and the general military membership were swallowing it whole. With Havana as the capital, funds were needed to maintain slavery through succession and conquest throughout the circle, from northern South America, Mexico, the southern US, and the Caribbean islands. There were many sympathizers in the north who supported this cause, which originated in Cincinnati.[1] Ebenezer Thorne, Virgil's father, had asked Virgil to take his place since he couldn't travel, being in his late 60's. Virgil didn't like the KGC and didn't like the people associated with it but his father had asked him to go and he heeded his wishes, taking the position his father had held for several years in the organization.

Members had come from throughout the south and, in a

private meeting, committed Virgil to collect and hide the gold needed to finance the KGC in the coming years. Talk of war was imminent and they all knew Eb Thorn would be able to stash gold where it couldn't be found. He had been using gold for years and no one knew where it came from—Except Virgil and Zack.

Riding away from the meeting hall, Zack said "How are they going to do it?"

"By rider, one bar per 5 riders," Virgil answered. "That will be 5 bars per state, each from Virginia, North Carolina, South Carolina, Georgia, and Tennessee. Other southern states, Louisiana, Missouri, Texas, and Arkansas, will go with Ohio, Pennsylvania, Kentucky, Indiana, and Illinois, and stash in the north."

"That's a lot of gold we will be holding," Zack said smiling. "Somewhere right around $200,000!"

"That's a lot of gold to be responsible for," Virgil added. "With our stash, we have to be extra careful".

"I agree," Zack responded.

"Those men in there have no idea what they are getting into. They are intelligent men swept up in this political ordeal and think they can succeed," said Virgil sarcastically. "We have our flanks exposed, not only because of political issues; now we have their state money, which is even more of a risk to our own."

"And the train poses even more of a threat. Should we continue with that operation?" Zach asked.

Virgil said emphatically "Yes. We must! It's the right thing to do. Runaways need to find their way north. Any way we can help, we need to. And, it's our cover with those up north. One thing we've learned is to never take sides and to play both sides at once. That way you are hated by both sides, but also respected by both sides."

"Or get lynched by both sides!" Zach added.

CHAPTER TWO

Virgil was born in 1818 on a plantation in eastern North Carolina. His father had begun, and prospered growing sweet potatoes, delivering them throughout the entire eastern seaboard. His plantation was over 2000 acres and he employed many slaves, purchased them, paid them, and freed many after an agreed amount of time of service. It was an indentured service of sorts. He did not believe in slavery, but kept it to himself and his family, not to upset the status quo. Many of the slaves stayed on the plantation as free workers since, other than Canada, there were limited places to go.

Virgil and Zack grew up together and were inseparable. Zack was 6 months younger than Virgil and his mother had wet-nursed Virgil as well. When they were 19, Ebenezer sent them both to Philadelphia for schooling. Zack enrolled in Cheyney College, founded in 1837, and the oldest predominantly African American institution of higher education in the US. It had started with monetary funds bequeathed by Richard Humphreys, a Quaker philanthropist.[1] Zack did extremely well; he was intelligent and well-educated, not normal for a black person from North Carolina. They both loved Philadelphia and the city life, especially Zack. The ability to walk freely throughout the streets and not be constantly on guard for tormentors was a joy. Not that he didn't have issues with some people, but not nearly as much as he would in North Carolina. Zack's social interests revolved around other local students' families and the social network they kept.

Virgil also loved Philadelphia; the hustle and bustle of a big city and large port. He spent many hours talking to seamen about where they had been and what they had seen. He also spent time talking to shipping owners regarding his father's plantation products and potential outlets in Europe.

One owner, Thaddeus Williams, had a daughter, Phoebe, with whom he fell madly in love. Phoebe was tall for the day, around 5'6", and had a thin, wiry frame. Her dark blonde curls fell to her shoulders and her blue eyes were penetrating. Her eyes were what Virgil first noticed, and when they locked onto his, he was mesmerized. Later, even Zack, in brotherly banter, told Virgil Phoebe's eyes could see through your body and your soul, and still put a smile on your face.

Thaddeus Williams had fought in the revolutionary war while his father had run the English blockade many times, supplying the army with sorely needed contraband. After the war, the shipping company thrived with new-found ports of call in many different countries.

Phoebe Williams was the youngest of four children born into Philadelphia society. With family wealth came status. Their family had grown exponentially, and her brothers and sister were all doing quite well as merchants. Phoebe was definitely the most spoiled of the children and was somewhat of a socialite in her father's eyes. Her intelligence and will were always a match for her parents and her older siblings. She was educated and knew how to navigate the business world as well as the social scene.

Virgil had seen her at several functions from a distance. She was attractive, but not stunning in most eyes. Virgil never had the opportunity to be introduced.

At one such social event, Virgil was walking the patio of a large house and entering the ballroom, when he literally bumped into

Phoebe, spilling his spiked punch all over his new, and expensive, suit. He was so embarrassed, he turned bright red.

Phoebe was a little amused by his flushing; she looked straight at him and profusely apologized for the incident. After absent-mindedly brushing off the liquid, he looked into her eyes for the first time... and melted. He stammered "Please excuse my clumsiness. I hope your dress has not been splashed." She replied, "No sir, I have not been soiled, unlike you. And, it is a pity to waste such," whispering, "dark rum punch." She and her friend both giggled while Virgil tried to compose himself.

What a beauty. He could tell she was smart and sophisticated. Those blue eyes, somewhat grayish, somewhat greenish in different lights. Her eyes were so dominant a feature, that looking elsewhere usually took time. She was aware of this reaction from most people and would fix her stare on whomever she met, long enough for them to completely absorb them, and then divert their own eyes. Her eyes penetrated Virgil's soul and he knew he was dealing with someone he had never encountered in his past dalliances.

He blushed again, and excused himself to clean the mess. That was their first introduction. He couldn't get her out of his mind. The whole next day he tried to discreetly find out who she was, but to no avail.

Two days later Virgil had a meeting with Thaddeus Williams to discuss possibly exporting sweet potatoes from Eastern North Carolina. Not only was his father growing them, but several other plantations also harvested the product. Finding other ports in the country would help all growers, and Mr. Williams had ships close in Elizabeth City, North Carolina, one of the major ports in the area. He sat in Mr. Williams' office for almost an hour, discussing the possible business, when the door opened and Phoebe strolled in.

Mr. Williams said, "I'm sorry dear, but I am in a meeting." Phoebe looked at him and responded, "Please excuse my interruption, father."

Then she looked at Virgil, paused only a second, and said "I hope your blouse and soiled outer garments came clean."

Stumbling to his feet to greet the intruder was clumsy. He gathered his wits quickly and decided to spar with this lady.

"My garments came clean. However, the white blouse is as stained as is my chest, and will take some time to come out." They both laughed while Mr. Williams stood somewhat confused.

"Father, I inadvertently bumped into this gentleman, but have never been formally introduced," Phoebe explained.

Mr. Williams introduced them and Virgil said, "In lieu of cleaning my garments, I would ask you to accompany me to visit your father's ships, if that is ok with your father?"

Mr. Williams agreed, liking this young man very much.

Phoebe responded, "Not that I'd ever clean your garments, I will accompany you down the wharf. You, in return, must buy me tea at our family's favorite tea house."

Virgil looked at Mr. Williams and said, "With your permission, sir?" At which, Mr. Williams looked at both of them bewildered. Not only was he overwhelmed by his daughter, but also was thrown from his own business meeting. He said, "Yes, of course. Phoebe, we will expect you for dinner at 7PM."

That evening before dinner, Mr. Williams told his wife "That girl has more nerve than anyone I have ever known. She may well be the death of me." Mrs. Williams replied "That girl will be the matriarch of this family one day. You need to trust her."

At 7PM, Phoebe came strolling into dinner, leading Virgil for a family introduction. Their relationship was off and running.

After six months of courtship, the issue became whether Phoebe would agree to marry him and move to North Carolina. Her social network in Philadelphia would be very hard to leave, as would her family and extended family. With her looks came an iron will that Virgil already knew well; once she put her mind to something, it was hard to change.

"Mr. Thorne," Phoebe started to say.

Virgil interrupted, "Phoebe, for God's sake."

"Mr. Thorne," Phoebe repeated in her best southern accent, "You have asked me to marry you. We have known each other for less than a year. You gallivant around the city with your college chums, and you prefer the company of a freed black man over mine," she continued wistfully. "How can I marry such a rogue?"

Phoebe could see right through Virgil and knew this would annoy him.

Virgil was definitely annoyed. "Phoebe stop! This is serious. I know I'd be taking you from your family and your friends and this really sits heavy on my mind."

"Virgil, calm down," Phoebe replied in her normal voice. "I love you and want to be with you. My sister and brothers all have their own lives and live close to Mama and Papa. Mama has been ill for a long time and my sister Ginny will watch over her. The house has been left to me. I'll have responsibilities here." The house was a large brick federal-style home about a half of a mile from the piers, built by Mr. Williams ten years before. It wasn't quite the mansion, but it was comparatively large for the city at that time.

"The summers in North Carolina are dreadfully hot," Phoebe continued. "As long as you are ok with me spending some of the summer here, I will gladly go to North Carolina with you. Granted, we will not keep slaves. I will not be a part of that culture."

Virgil agreed on all points. She was the person he had always dreamt of. She and Virgil were very much in love and she agreed to marry him. The wedding was held in Philadelphia and the entire Thorne clan and their social network was in attendance. When they relocated to North Carolina, another grand reception was held for the newlyweds.

As much as Zack wanted to stay in Philadelphia, he simply couldn't leave his family or Virgil. So, at the mature age of 21, they both returned to the plantation life in North Carolina; and Virgil with a new wife.

Chapter Three

Several times a year, it was Virgil's responsibility to take the harvest of sweet potatoes to market. Their main outlet was the port in Elizabeth City, which delivered to northern cities. They also delivered to Richmond and Fredericksburg in Virginia. Both had busy ports but their main customers delivered to the western regions of the state, Washington D.C., and northern cities, including Baltimore and Philadelphia.

On one such trip, both Virgil and Zack drove and were accompanied by several other heavy wagons pulled by large draft horses that could pull up to 4000 pounds. That trip was headed for Fredericksburg. After unloading and during their overnight stay, Virgil had been regaled with stories of the gold mines in Spotsylvania, Fauquier, and Louisa Counties.

A miner told him that he had been working a stream called the Rapidan River and had found plenty of nuggets and dust in the stream bed.

"I'm telling you," the miner told him. "There is gold there in those stream beds but not enough to find the source. As the heavier gold falls to the bottom of the stream, it has to be coming from somewhere."

"You are full of it," his partner retorted. "That gold has been there for years and any source is long gone!"

"Let me buy you a drink and you explain it all to me," Virgil responded; which was all he needed to say. The miners had been filing claims and moving from place to place looking for good spots where the sand and gravel gave easily. Some had sluices; most panned.

"You recommend panning and finding good nuggets before erecting a sluice?" Asked Virgil.

"That's right," said the first miner. "Some guys dig into the ground but no one has found anything of value. Plus, digging and hammering rock is not what I signed up for."

"If you found gold in solid rock, you'd be digging it. Who are you fooling?" His partner reacted.

This went on for a half hour and eventually Virgil was intrigued enough to think about it.

After mulling it over the next day with Zack, Virgil sent the other wagons back to North Carolina, while he and Zack headed about 15 miles west to Spotsylvania to investigate these claims of gold mines.

They encountered some farms and a couple of small hamlets. However, the region was heavily deforested and the undergrowth became a dense tangle. Very few people lived there except for a few farms. At the confluence of the Rappahannock and Rapidan rivers they met a couple of miners who said they had been finding dust in the streams, but nothing very large.

On the Rapidan River, they met two miners who were leaving, saying their claims produced some gold but had run out.

"How's the prospecting been," Virgil asked them. A young man in his late twenties replied "We've just about cleared the riverbed of any dust. There was some, about 2 ounces worth. Enough to keep us going. We're moving downstream. Heard there's plenty more."

Zack whispered to Virgil, "In college I studied some geology and included in those courses was information on gold. Gold is heavy and sinks. It falls."

Virgil said "I know. I had some courses also and know that most streams are fed by smaller streams."

"Exactly," Zack said. "Look at that small stream coming from underneath that rock outcrop. Any gold would come down that stream and land in the stream bed here. The gold is in there, not here."

"You boys want to sell this claim?" Virgil asked the miners.

"Sure," said the young man. "How much do you have?" "Not much," Virgil replied, "but I'll give you 30 dollars for it, all 10 acres."

"Sold!" Said the other man. "That's the best profit we've made so far."

They sold their claim to Virgil and said he'd have to register it in Spotsylvania.

After camping at the site for the night, the next day Virgil rode to the Spotsylvania Courthouse and filed the land sale. When he returned in the late afternoon, Zack had already started digging around to see where they would begin their mining. They both thought starting near the rock outcrop would be the most suitable place to sink a shaft.

So they did. After a month of digging, they went in about ten feet, and about eight feet high and four feet wide, enough to get in and use a pickaxe. At ten feet in they hit solid rock.

Finally, chipping away at the rock, they found trace evidence of gold at eleven feet. A week later, at twelve feet in, they hit a vein of gold that released a nugget that weighed at least fifteen pounds—A nugget, very little quartz, pyrite, or other elements. A somewhat pure nugget. The vein looked to run about two feet across and back into the rock. They had hit the mother lode.

The next few days, they spent making a crude cabin on the flat next to the mine entrance. The gold they dug from the rock weighed close to 1000 pounds, a half ton of the purest gold they had ever seen. It took almost another month to get to the end of the vein. And then it was gone. No shining or trace, nothing.

But they were beside themselves. Over 1000 pounds of gold

would be enough to live on for the rest of their lives. They talked endlessly about what the next moves would be, how they would spend it. Then they realized turning in that much gold would create issues with the local government, politicians, lawyers, thieves, anyone who would like to take the gold from them. They decided they really had only one choice on how to proceed. But they still had two problems: One, and the more important, they had been gone close to three months and Virgil knew Phoebe would be furious with him being away so long with little word. Zack's fiancé, Sarah, was as smart and strong-willed as Phoebe. They had sent a couple of letters to let them know they were ok. But they both knew digging for gold, instead of taking care of the plantation, would not only anger their bride and beau, but also Eb Thorne. Virgil knew his father well enough. After the growing season and harvest, there was a down time, but it only lasted a couple of months. He would be looking for them to return shortly.

Secondly, how to get over 1000 pounds of gold home and in the state, in a way that would not raise speculation or robbery attempts enroute? They came up with a plan.

There was a local businessman named John Wellford, who, with partners, had built a furnace in Spotsylvania. Catharine furnace, named after Wellford's mother, had begun operation several years before and was making pig iron for iron works in Fredericksburg and Richmond. Virgil had met Wellford in a local tavern and had been introduced by other businessmen in the area.[1] Wellford had called him the "sweet potato man." They all loved Virgil's sweet potatoes in the region.

He rode to the furnace and asked to speak to Mr. Wellford, who not only was the primary investor, but also the general manager. Mr. Wellford greeted him cordially.

Virgil opened by saying, "Mr. Wellford, I have a business proposition for you." Mr. Wellford showed him into his office and closed the door.

"What can I do for you, young man?"

Virgil said "after delivering the last couple of wagons of sweet potatoes to Fredericksburg, my friend Zack Washington and I heard stories and ventured into the gold mining area of the county. Zack and I bought a claim, about ten acres of land on the lower Rapidan River."

"I see," said Mr. Wellford. "Go on."

"Well, we have been fortunate. What I am proposing is to rent your furnace for 48 hours to melt down what we have into bars to transport," Virgil said softly. He added, "this is a very delicate matter of which I will take only you into my confidence."

Mr. Wellford's eyes widened as he said, "You have found that much gold?"

"Yes and no," Virgil replied. "We have found enough to smelt maybe 2-3 bars, enough to change the look of the gold, instead of carrying dust and nuggets in bags. It would also make transporting much easier and less conspicuous. For the use of the furnace, we'll pay you five pounds in dust and nuggets."

Mr. Wellford took a minute to scribble on a piece of paper, and then looked up surprised and said, "That's over $1200. That is a lot of money to use the forge for really one day."

"That is a lot of money to use the forge for one day and two nights, and really to buy your silence." Virgil responded. "We are scared that if word got out that we had three bars of gold, something may happen. Can I trust you, Mr. Wellford?"

"My boy," he started, "for $1200 I'll wear a gag for two weeks."

Virgil said, "So, we have an agreement?"

Mr. Wellford was ecstatic. "Of course," he blurted. "Come by Saturday morning and I'll personally show you how it's done. I have small ingots for lead that are perfect, and also sodium carbonate and sodium borate for the large crucible to burn out any impurities. I know you don't understand what I'm talking about, but I'll show you on Saturday. It's really a simple process, but it can get very hot and dangerous at those temperatures."

"Deal," Virgil thanked him. "And we will be very careful."

On Thursday and Friday, Zack and Virgil purchased lumber to make a false bottom on the wagon. The idea was ingenious. They did such a good job, no one would be able to see anything underneath or in between the lumber. They stashed all of the large nuggets and bags of nuggets there before riding to the furnace. Mr. Wellford would only see several large bags in the rear covered by canvas and other supplies.

True to his word, on Saturday afternoon, Mr. Wellford met them at the guard house and showed them to the main furnace. He explained in detail how to melt the ore and how much of the chemicals to use per pound. Zack had been in town purchasing the lumber and had also purchased both sodium borate and sodium carbonate from the local chemist, all he could get. He knew they'd need extra. When he explained to the chemist it was for Mr. Wellford's operation, no eyebrows were raised. Mr. Wellford would see how much of the chemicals would have been used and deduce the amount of gold that was smelted. This way he would not be suspicious of the little amount consumed.

He posted a guard at the guardhouse with instructions to keep people out and not venture into the furnace area. The young negro would do as he was told, or face the consequences.

After quitting time and with everyone gone, Zack gave the ok "You ready?" Virgil replied, "Make sure the furnace is over 2000 degrees and I'll back the wagon into the furnace area."

That night and into the next night they loaded the gold into the huge crucible, melted the ore, poured the gold into four ingots, cooled them, and repeated the process eight to nine times. When they were finished, they had 42 bars that weighed 25 pounds each. It was worth over $250,000 (over $30 million in today's value). They hid the bars and two bags of dust in the false bottom of the wagon. They kept three bars and one bag of nuggets and dust in the wagon. Three bags weighed five pounds and one bag weighed six pounds. They slept for a couple of hours and, bright and early on Monday morning, Mr. Wellford came to see the results. Like promised, Virgil handed him a bag. He was in awe of the gold and when he saw three bars, he about had a heart attack.

"Mr. Wellford," Virgil announced, "I won't be needing the 10 acres I bought from that other miner. You have been good to us, so I'm going to deed that property to you as additional payment."

"You boys have done well. I wish you all of the luck in the world. And thank you for this generous payment. Your secret is safe with me! By the way, did the mine play out?"

"That's why we are leaving," Zack replied. "It was a good but small vein."

"Too bad," Mr. Wellford responded. "I'm sure there is more out there somewhere. Stop by the next time you deliver sweet potatoes!"

With that, they said their goodbyes and started towards Fredericksburg. They stopped at Spotsylvania Courthouse and deeded the 10 acres of property to Mr. Wellford. In Fredericksburg, they turned in one bag to the government buyer, who paid them with script. That is what most miners did when they sold the dust. The gold was used in the mints in the north to make coins. Virgil then purchased five farm bales of tobacco to fill the wagon and not return empty-handed. They also purchased two handguns and a shotgun, just to be safe.

On the Richmond Road, going was easier than county travel and had much more traffic. Once in Richmond, Virgil rented a room at an inn and Zack slept in the stable with the horses and the wagon. He teased Virgil about having the comfort of a nice bed and sheets after the months spent at the mine. They both knew the less suspicion that was raised, the safer they would be.

The next morning, they stopped by the government office and sold the last two bags of dust for more script. They wanted to keep one bar for Virgil's father just to show they weren't making things up. The total they had now was over $4000. The plan was for both of them to buy property and build houses. They had sworn secrecy to each other regarding their stash of gold. Virgil would help Zack hide the stash, but he told him he would definitely tell Phoebe about it, and Zack would tell Sarah. They had to know about it, but *not* know where it would be hidden. That step was taken to keep Phoebe and Sarah safe in case of any future trouble.

CHAPTER FOUR

Ebenezer Thorne was alerted to his son's return long before they approached the house. As they pulled around back towards the stables, Eb was standing on the back porch watching them. Virgil and Zack both knew what that meant.

They entered his study on the main floor still with road dust on their old, tattered clothes. They had bought supplies, but had not bought any new clothing.

As they closed the door and stood in front of the big oak desk, Eb blurted, "Where are the proceeds from the sale, where have you been for almost four months, and why do you look like you do?" Zack started to ease towards the door and Eb said "Not so fast, Zack. You have explaining to do too. Your folks have worried me to death and Sarah is beside herself."

Virgil said, "Papa, we sold the harvest and headed into Spotsylvania County outside of Fredericksburg because we heard they were finding gold in the streams there."

Eb rose from his seat "You went looking for gold? All of the education for you both I have paid, and you come up with..." At Eb's mid-sentence, Virgil slapped a 25-pound bar of pure gold on the desk that he had kept in a canvas bag by his side. The clunk sounded as if it would go right through the desktop. Eb stood up open-mouthed and asked, "Is that real?"

Zack said, "Yes, and there is one more."

Virgil added, "As soon as we get cleaned and changed, we have a proposition for you."

"We have to hide those," was Eb's immediate response. Both Virgil and Zack said at the same time, "We know." Eb quickly put it in his desk's bottom drawer, looked up at them and smiled; a smile they both loved and told them he was proud of them. "We'll talk later. Both of you have some explaining to do to the womenfolk."

As Virgil left the room, he was accosted by his mother, and right behind her was Phoebe, who stared through him. He recovered quickly from that piercing look and produced a smile so broad Phoebe was instantly disarmed. Then he looked down and saw the bulge in Phoebe's dress. He almost started to cry.

In her best southern accent, Phoebe said, "Mr. Thorne, you have some answering to do;" to which Virgil replied, "Mrs. Thorne, you are the dearest sight I have ever encountered." He put his hand on her stomach, kissed her on the cheek, and whispered in her ear, "a dearer sight than even the gold we found." Her whole face showed pure surprise; eyes wide, mouth agape, she could not believe what she had just heard. Virgil continued, "I know now you are the dearest treasure I could ever have. And now, the treasure will multiply."

Phoebe interrupted him, "Wait. What did you just say? And forget the sweet talk."

"Let's go into our room and I'll tell you all about it," Virgil responded.

Once in their room, Virgil recounted the whole story and Phoebe listened without a pause. After she mulled for a moment, she said, "Virgil, no one can find out and you have to hide that gold."

Virgil said, "I know. Zack and I talked long and hard about what to do and we came up with a plan. You have to remember that half of that gold is Zack's. How we use it and cash it in is going to be very tricky all around."

"Where will you hide it?" Phoebe asked.

"Wherever we decide, we will never tell you or Sarah for the simple reason that, if anything bad were ever to happen, neither of you would be pressured to divulge its whereabouts. We need to keep you both safe."

"I don't know, Virgil," Phoebe responded. "Seems as though you want to keep it from me."

"Not at all," he replied. "You can have as much as you want whenever you want it. It's yours. It's ours. It will never come between us, but you can always say you have no idea where any gold is kept, and anyone trying to get information out of you will not be able to, since you won't have that information. Think about it and if you really disagree, we'll discuss it further. I will not let it come between us. I promise."

Virgil continued, "Since our family is about to grow, what do you think about building a house on the 50 acres Papa has across the river from Edenton? It's only about two miles from the house, we'll have our privacy, and we'll have access to town by boat, like we do now. Yet our lives will be separate from any prying eyes. Zack wants the 20 acres next to it, so we'll be close."

"Virgil, if you can't trade in gold, how will you pay for a house?"

"Don't worry about Papa. He has been compensated," Virgil responded, while he pulled out the money from the bags of gold nuggets and dust they had cashed in. Once again, Phoebe's eyes widened and her mouth opened wide.

"Mrs. Thorne, that look is very unbecoming of a lady," Virgil teased.

"Mr. Thorne, I always thought you were a rogue. Now I am convinced of it," Phoebe responded in her southern accent.

They kissed and hugged, content for the time being.

They threw themselves into the design and construction of their new home. The newfound fortune gave the opportunity to not spare expense in construction of the house. With the abundance of clay and oyster shells in the region, quality brick and mortar was readily available. Each room would have a large fireplace, solid oak floors from planks brought from the western mountains, imported English glass for the windows, a leaded stained glass window for the attic window, a full basement, and a kitchen that boasted a fireplace large enough to entertain any number of guests they wanted to invite. Local workers were hired for most of the construction. For the intricate work, artisans from large cities were brought in for the wood carvings and glass applications. And an engineer that Tyler and Zack knew from Philadelphia came for almost a month and helped with the construction.

Months later, they were proud of the prestige their new home gave them. Visitors from the area marveled at the craftsmanship and amount of money they poured into the construction and furnishing of the house. For the time, the house had no equal in quality. Before it was completed, their son Tyler was born and Phoebe was due with their second child shortly thereafter. Having four bedrooms was going to be needed and was a good decision. Their family was growing.

Zack and Virgil both worked on Zack's house, which was basically next door. Zack did not construct his house in quite the same manner as Virgil did. However, it was solidly built and large enough to accommodate his growing family. Zack married Sarah and she was expecting their first child.

The two couples spent much of their free time together. Phoebe and Sarah grew very fond of each other and supported each other with their growing families. It was uncommon for the time, but the locals knew how close the families were and accepted the fact that Virgil and Zack were just like brothers. Phoebe and Sarah knew the secret and shared their common apprehension with their spouses, but that secret never came between any of them.

CHAPTER FIVE

The KGC had sent the gold they had promised. Each state had their state logo and emblem etched into the gold bars that were delivered, since they came from state coffers. How these men were able to secure state gold was nothing more than a miracle. But each person in the KGC was an upstanding citizen in their respective states, so getting the gold was not difficult.

It arrived at different times at the plantation, where Zack was already waiting. He hid the bars in the same wagon he and Virgil had used eighteen years before. Once they were all accounted for, Zack hid them in their secret hiding place when everyone in the area was in church, on Sunday morning.

While sitting on the front porch sipping iced tea, Zack commented, "I don't like those men at all. Your papa has a different outlook from all of them, yet he still is a part of their circle."

The ladies joined them on the porch then, after shooing off several playing children who followed them outside. Upon seeing them, Virgil addressed them, "Ladies, you need to be part of this conversation. The KGC has entrusted us with gold from the coffers of different states, five in total. This puts us in a sticky state of affairs."

Sarah replied in a stern tone, "I don't like it. We are helping a lot of folks get north and now you and Zack have put us out there for others to come looking around. And our children are right in the middle of it."

"Now Sarah," Zack tried to stop her.

"Don't you 'Now Sarah' me, Zachariah Washington" she shot back, mimicking him. Both Virgil and Phoebe laughed at her imitation.

Next, it was Phoebe's turn to do her best imitation of Virgil, "Zack, why you always get on the wrong side of the horse?"

Virgil, imitating Zack, said "Cause that's how I do it."

They all laughed together and Zack reacted, "I can imitate you just as well, Virgil!"

They sat laughing even harder on that balmy afternoon, two couples who had truly grown to love one another over time; not only each other, but also each other's children, and their extended families. Everyone around knew how close they all were. However, their relationship always raised suspicion from the old southerners who didn't like the idea of free blacks mingling with white families.

Phoebe added, "Sarah is right, Zack. We need an alternative plan if things go wrong."

"There could be a war soon and we need a plan to safeguard our families," Virgil said. "The gold doesn't matter at this point." He paused slightly, "Well, it does matter for our future and our children's futures. But for now, if we do go to war, our families' safety is our primary concern. So, I say, let's use Philadelphia as a contingency, and move what we need to Philadelphia as a safeguard."

They all agreed. The plan was to secretly transport bars to Phoebe's father's house, where it would be safe. Phoebe's mother had passed and her father was getting older; Phoebe was spending more time with him. Sarah had accompanied Phoebe with all five of their combined children to his house many times over the years, and Mr. Williams thoroughly enjoyed everyone's company. The house was big enough for all of them and he welcomed the chaos that grandchildren brought. He loved spoiling them all.

Tyler, Virgil and Phoebe's oldest son, was soon to be sixteen. He had spent summers with his grandparents and loved Philadelphia, just like his father. Plans were made for him to enroll in college there, in a year or so, just as his father had done. Phoebe would take two bars with her when she next traveled north, along with Tyler. They would travel by ship out of Elizabeth City to Philadelphia, so as to be safer than overland or by train.

She traveled three times between 1858 and 1860, all three times with Sarah. Her father had moved from his upstairs bedroom to a bedroom on the first floor, to avoid having to navigate the stairs. Phoebe set up the master bedroom as her own and was able to hide the gold bars in a false wall she and Sarah had built into one of the bedroom closets. Later, once in Philadelphia, she would not have any issues changing the gold into cash. She had outlets in Philadelphia, New York, and Boston that would exchange the gold with no questions asked. The government needed as much gold as they could get after the war to pay debts.

CHAPTER SIX

In January of 1861, Ebenezer Thorne passed away quietly in his sleep. Virgil's mother would not be able to manage the plantation. She would not see the end of the year herself, also passing away quietly in her sleep. The decision was made for Virgil and his family to move into the big house, and Zack and his family moved into the house overlooking the river, which Virgil had built. Zack kept the smaller house and twenty acres, and rented that property.

The war began that spring and North Carolina was the next-to-last state to join the Confederacy. In late 1861, Elizabeth City fell to Union Gunboats and New Bern eventually did the following year. The entire eastern seaboard was blockaded and under Union control. Only Wilmington held out towards the end of the war.

During the war, Virgil's plantation was left alone, producing a food crop that both the Northern armies and the local people needed to sustain life. The crops were needed by everyone. Virgil was 'dancing the fence,' as Zack called it.

During the winter of 1865, General Sherman was marching north and burning everything in his path. General Joseph Johnston was trapped in Raleigh and General Robert E Lee was under siege in Petersburg. Edenton was far enough away from the fighting, but was still under union control. At this point, the union army was huge, over 60,000 men spread out throughout the state, but eventually would converge in Bentonville, southeast of Raleigh. Union "Bummers" scoured the entire state for provisions to feed the army. Sherman's supply lines were secure at this point, but the Bummers were still in scouring mode about the countryside for as much food as they could find. It served to feed the army, but also kept food sources away from the confederate army; and it served to make the local population feel the sting of war and rebellion—Sherman's famous "Make the South Howl" campaign.[1]

Prior to this time, the 'train' had increased dramatically. Once the union troops moved north into North Carolina, there was little need. Most freed slaves stayed with the army. A growing problem of feeding and sheltering close to 5000 people was a constant hindrance to the movement of the federals.[2]

On a cold March morning, Virgil was in his study with two of his farm hands reviewing field allocations, when they heard riders approaching the house. Virgil looked out his study window and saw union soldiers approaching the house on horseback accompanied by wagons. He knew what it meant; however, these didn't look like the troops he normally saw. They all had different hats and wore articles of clothing not part of the usual uniform. The hair on the back of his neck raised, as he knew there could be trouble.

Virgil turned to Sam, one of the planters, and said "Sam, those aren't normal soldiers. They are bummers. Run through the house and get my family out of here. Take them to Zack's immediately. Just overcoats and shoes, nothing else." Everyone knew who bummers were and how ruthless they could be. News of Sherman's march was everywhere, and everyone feared running into any of his troops. The psychological effects of his tactics absolutely worked.

Sam sped off through the house. He told Phoebe, "Bummers at the front door." Phoebe knew the drill and grabbed the two children, shoes, overcoats, and silently went out through the kitchen door. As she looked back, she saw Virgil on the front porch talking to the soldiers. Virgil looked back through the open door and locked eyes with Phoebe—for the last time.

They ran through the yard and behind the barn until they entered the woods. The walk to Zack's house was over two miles and they started the journey cold, scared, and full of fear for their husband and father. Sam ran the entire 2 miles ahead to tell Zack what was going on.

Once the news spread, Zack told Sam to gather all of the local families and meet at his house. The union soldiers would not burn or plunder a house that had slaves living in it. Zack saddled his horse and sped to the plantation house.

The barn was on fire and Zack could smell the smoke before he could see it. As he approached through the front gate, the house was also burning. He found Virgil in front of the steps of the front porch, on the ground, next to household items that had been ransacked. A bullet had gone straight through his heart. Zack screamed and let out a moan that he didn't know was in him. His brother, his soulmate, lay dead in his arms.

PART TWO
PRESENT DAY

CHAPTER SEVEN

The house was in bad shape. The roof boards were warped, the front porch sagged, paint was peeling everywhere on the house. The front yard hadn't been mowed in years—if you could call it a front yard. Weeds and thickets surrounded the house proper; it was not known what was growing up the one chimney. And that was just the outside.

Tyler Harrington had bought the house unseen. The realtor had assured him the property needed work. He wanted it, no matter what.

"Mr. Harrington," Jimmy Knox, the realtor, said, "I hope you are not as shocked as I think you might be."

Tyler replied, "Not at all, Mr. Knox," showing his coolness under pressure. He always had the ability to not show his emotions or let anyone else know his thoughts through facial expressions. "I knew it was going to take a lot of work," he added.

But damn, this place was a wreck. No matter, it is what he had signed up for and what he wanted to do.

Jimmy went on, "The electricity is on in our real estate company's name. You'll have to change that as soon as the title switches. At your request, we verified the well is safe, and the pump is working. It is old and I'm not sure how long it will last. We had them tested last week. The home inspection company listed all of the issues with the house and the property, including the small barn. The water is working, but the plumbing is inadequate, as is the water pressure. You do have a working commode and kitchen sink. Not sure about the bathing facilities at this point. As you know, the heat is from a radiator, and there is an old oil burner in the basement. It is working now, but again, not sure for how long. All of this is listed in your information packet. If you remember, these charges were included in the closing costs."

"Of course," replied Tyler. "I appreciate you and your company going the extra mile for me. It was very accommodating."

Jimmy replied, "We do aim to please. It's a small town and any word of your satisfaction with our service will go a long way. Plus, a lot of the locals needed extra work. You may find that comes in handy with what you are about to undertake."

Tyler said "I do, and I will talk around town about your excellent service. Thank you!"

Jimmy handed him the keys and said, "The gold key is the front door, the silver key the back door, and the green key is to the barn. I sincerely wish you well, Mr. Harrington. If you need anything from me, please do not hesitate to call. We are a small community."

After Jimmy left, Tyler wanted to walk around the house to see the rest of the property. There were ten acres, mainly to the back of the house and down to the river. Tyler walked around the side of the house and the first thing he noticed through the bare trees was the gentle slope to the water. The house had been built on one of the very few knolls along the river. He made a mental note to look for the house from across the river. Edenton was just there, a little south, and was in somewhat plain view through the tops of the trees. He imagined that if he stood on the roof of the house, he'd have a clear view across the river. He was very satisfied with that thought.

As he rounded the corner at the back of the house, he noticed, on the far side, the largest tree stump he had ever seen, starting about ten feet from the house. It was a white oak stump that had to be at least eight to ten feet wide, leaning towards the water and away from the house. There had to be a story behind that tree. And there was, as he would later find out.

The barn, which looked more like a small stable, had a door with a padlock on it. The door looked as though it was the only part of the entire structure that remained sound. A strong wind might push the entire barn over and down the hill. It had to be over 100 years old and would have to be demolished. There was no saving it in his mind. Whole sections of the roof and some of the sides were gone. He made a mental note: new barn.

Continuing around the house, the brick was in good shape. The mortar needed some touching up and general cleaning. But there were no apparent weaknesses. The windows, on the other hand, looked original or replaced in the early 1900's. Caulking was eroded and the sills and sashes looked rotted. He made another mental note: new roof and new windows to start.

Moving up onto the porch, which creaked and seemed to give way as he walked on it, he looked inside the window next to the front door, but could not see anything through the dirt and grime on the glass. The door was in good shape, definitely having been replaced sometime in the last 50 years.

Entering the front foyer, Tyler was pleasantly surprised at the condition of the hallway and front rooms. They were livable, or really inhabitable. There was much cleaning and sanitation needed on the floors, walls, and ceiling. Cobwebs, dust, and dirt were very evident, but it was not an overwhelming job; a couple of days of cleaning, and he would be able to stay in the house.

The foyer was wide and open, leading to the kitchen. To the right was a staircase that went upstairs to the bedrooms. Before the stairwell, there was a doorway leading to a formal living area that was more of a parlor than a living room. To the left of the foyer was the great room/dining room/entertainment room. It was larger than the parlor and extended the length of the hallway.

On the outside wall of each of the front rooms was a fireplace with a mantle. Both were well used and were probably something special in their day. Tyler quickly looked at his information packet and searched for the page describing the status of the fireplaces. All were in working order and had been swept/cleaned. The fireplace on the wall of the back room opposite the kitchen needed work done on the top of the chimney, with loose brick and mortar. All needed chimney caps. The four chimneys in the house were a sign that the original owners were well to do and could afford to build a house in which every room had a fireplace. Not that they were really needed in North Carolina. It rather seemed like an apparent status symbol.

Tyler moved through the great room, through a swinging door and into the kitchen. Now this is where he really got excited. The kitchen was large, spacious, and had a huge fireplace on the outside wall; one where cooks of old had hung cast iron pots and skillets over the fire and cooked meals. The brick front and sides were a good 2-3 feet into the room and it overshadowed anything else in the kitchen. The cast iron hooks were still on their swivels. It was the focal point. It was comfortable and, as a chef, Tyler was over-whelmed with excitement. He could already see the kitchen remodeled to his liking, still keeping the fireplace and its capabilities as the focal point of the room.

There was also a bathroom next to the rooms on the right, in between the parlor and what looked like a study, which leant meaning to the term *water closet*. It was as big as a closet and only contained an antique commode and antique wall-mounted wash basin that crowded the commode.

Behind the study was a room that was used for washing, what we'd call a mud room, or washer and dryer room, no plumbing of course. At the end of the main hallway, in between the kitchen and mudroom was a back door that led outside. Before reaching the back door was an open stairwell that led up on one side. On the opposite side, there was a larger stairwell that went down into the basement through a now closed door.

Tyler went upstairs first. The large front stairwell in the foyer creaked as he stepped up, and each stair sung its own tune. He was amused. The banister was solid and had an ornate knob at the bottom and top of the rail. The opposite wall had no rail, which he knew he would need to add.

The upstairs area was basically divided into four rooms, with one prior bedroom converted into a bathroom, in the middle back of the upstairs. The main stairs went up the right side and made a turn to the left, to a small hallway about six feet wide, and ended at the door to the big bedroom and the door to the bedroom behind it. There were two doors on the left and three doors on the right, with the bathroom door in the middle. There was a narrow hallway with a second door leading into the bathroom on the left, and another bedroom door on the right. The hallway led to the back stairs.

Each room had a fireplace and mantle that was very well constructed and, in the largest room, was quite ornate. Each hearth shared a chimney with the fireplace directly below it. The floorboards were made of hand-hewn oak and had very little creaking. The entire upstairs was solid and, aside from dust and cobwebs, needed only minor work on the walls and ceilings. Some of the radiators had small leak stains around their bases, easily sanded out, but no real water damage.

There were two doors on the right, leading to the bedrooms, a third door on the left of the narrow hallway entering the bathroom, and a fourth, smaller door, opposite the hallway leading to the attic, next to the main stairwell. Going up into the attic, he was greeted with old dusty air and very little insulation. Since most of the roof boards needed replacing, he would make sure the attic was redone with a new floor and a walled enclosure in the middle. One of the main beams was in need of major repair. Once completed, he would have room for a furnace and AC, and plenty of storage. There was a window at one end of the attic that was round and contained ornate stained glass; it was a beautiful throw to the past.

The basement had a couple of lone light bulbs that showed dimly the way around. The stairs were not stable and Tyler made another mental note as to immediate construction needs. The basement had a dirt floor with massive stone walls that gave the entire structure its ability to withstand the passage of time. It was dry and had a musty smell, but not moldy, which was a relief. There were some empty tins and boxes laying around, and a wooden shelving unit on the right wall. On the left wall was an old oil boiler that fed the radiators that ran throughout the house. Tyler made yet another mental note: new furnace and ductwork for air conditioning. He decided he would put another furnace and air conditioner in the attic to heat and cool the upstairs, again running ductwork while the roof was being replaced.

Back upstairs, he decided to start writing down his thoughts on needed tasks, before he forgot them, and put them somewhat in the order they would need to be accomplished. Changing electrical, plumbing, and HVAC always needed permits and decided he would need a contractor to help with those issues. First and foremost, he would have to clean the house to make it livable, then start chipping away at the reconstruction of his new home.

All in all, he was happy with his investment. The house was very old and needed a good amount of work. However, it was solidly built and was definitely more than salvageable.

CHAPTER EIGHT

Tyler drove into town and rented a hotel room for the next couple of days. It was getting colder in late November and staying in a hotel room seemed like a good idea for now, at least until he knew he had enough heat in the house to stay there. The moving truck was scheduled to arrive in the next two days and he knew that the heirloom furniture he was putting into the house would not come close to filling it. His small house outside Philadelphia was crammed with his and his parents' furniture. This much larger house would dwarf the furniture he had, but it would be enough for now. The essentials were coming —kitchen table, sofa and chair with two end tables, and two bedroom sets that would fill at least two of the bedrooms. If he could get the heat working, the plan was to move in the same day the furniture arrived.

The next morning, he hired a cleaning company to clean the inside of the house from top to bottom. They were available and could send four people that afternoon and the following day. Tyler went to the hardware store and purchased all imaginable cleaning supplies that he would need moving forward— buckets, brooms, mops, rags, cleaning chemicals, garbage bins; the list was large.

There was no need for any huge trash removal, but he knew the landscaping would need work, which he wanted to do himself.

Having a pickup truck in North Carolina is not only functional, but it also serves a cultural purpose. All right-minded Tar Heels have pick-up trucks. Tyler also decided to purchase rakes, shovels, hedge clippers, a weed eater, lawnmower, and other small tools needed for the normal household.

The young man at the hardware store looked at Tyler and asked, "You're planning some work, aren't you?" Tyler replied, "Yes sir. The more, the merrier."

Work was never an issue with Tyler. He thrived on chaos and juggling five jobs at once. As a celebrated chef in Eastern PA, Tyler had a great future. Then, one after another, things fell apart like dominoes lined up ready for the first one to knock over the rest, cascading until no upright dominoes remained.

That is why he gave up everything and purchased this house as far from Philadelphia as he could get. He loved Philadelphia, the city, the bustle, and the people; but he had to get away from memories that were too hard to think of, to remember, to relive.

He packed everything up in his cart and went to his truck, loading all the tools and equipment in the back —What a haul. He had never purchased so many items from a hardware store in his life. It was such a good feeling not having to worry about anything except the next bush to trim, the next wall to fix, or the next plumbing leak to mend. Mindless activity is what he needed and what he would pursue for the next several months, not so much trying to forget the past, but rather not to relive the pain he had endured over the last two years.

CHAPTER NINE

Early the next day, Tyler had to navigate the courthouse to start the permit process. He had to navigate the departments while the entire courthouse complex was being remodeled. There was scaffolding on the building exterior, sidewalks were torn up to be replaced with brick, and concrete was being poured in three different places.

After making his way into the building, he needed first to make sure that his deed was recorded at Land Records and the Registrar of Deeds. Next, it would be planning and inspections, and the tax department. Most of this information is now online. However, some counties do provide packets of information for purchase and remodeling of a non-commercial dwelling.

In his last stop at the tax department, he was greeted by an attractive lady whose name tag read "Barbara." She was writing something on her desk when Tyler approached her.

"Excuse me, Barbara," he said, looking at her name tag.

"Yes," she looked up absently. Immediately her eyes locked on to his and she was slightly taken aback for a second. She gathered herself and said, "My word, I have never seen such pretty eyes before." Tyler got this comment all of the time and had developed a way of returning a compliment that would shift focus onto his flatterer, rather than have to explain himself.

He said "They are from my mother's side. But I would guess you get the same compliment all of the time!"

Barbara didn't miss a beat. "No sir, flattery is usually saved for the perfect size and shape of my breasts," as she hiked them and showed them off. "My husband Craig used to get upset. But now, after two kids, he considers it somewhat of a trophy, if you get my drift."

Tyler liked this woman immediately. She made the comment with sincerity, humor, and with genuine, disarming nonchalance.

"He is one lucky man," Tyler responded, "and I'll make sure that if we ever meet, I'll let him know."

"Oh, he'd love that," Barbara responded. "Now, how can I help you, other than finding out who you are and everything about you. Just so you know, I know everyone and everything that is going on around here. In a couple of years, when my kids grow up, I'll be running the county, you mark my words."

Her accent was charming and Tyler couldn't help but like this woman. She was definitely a busy-body, but she didn't act facetious or too overbearing.

"My name is Tyler Harrington and I..." She cut him off in midsentence. "You just bought the Washington property".

"The Washington property?" Tyler said with a quizzical look on his face.

Barbara responded "Yes, the Washington place."

"You must be mistaken. I bought a property from the estate of a gentleman named Johnson," Tyler responded.

Barbara countered matter-of-factly, "Around here, once you purchase a property, the property is known by the last name of the last person that purchased the property. Mr. Johnson bought that property from the Washington family some 25 years ago. The house was owned by the Washington family for well over 100 years. So, he purchased the Washington property. However, he never really moved into it because he had bought the land as an investment, with no real desire to move here. Since he never moved here, the place was never considered the Johnson house; everyone still called it the Washington house. I told you I know everything," she continued with a smile. "Tax records flow through this office and a lien check is always done before a deed can be released. I saw your deed come through a couple of days ago."

Tyler was amused to learn something about the south he never knew. He didn't know houses were named. In Philadelphia, there were only street addresses.

She continued, after taking a breath, "What are your plans for the old place?"

Tyer decided to have some fun with her. He leaned toward her and said in a low voice "Don't tell anyone, but I'm going to remodel it and run rum up here from the islands!"

She looked at him and said in a whispered voice "You... are full of dog doodie!"

They both laughed. Tyler continued, "I *am* going to remodel it, move here, and hope that someday it will be known as the Harrington house."

She laughed again. "You catch on quick!" and added without taking a breath, "Are you really going to remodel it? That place has been vacant for so long it may not come around."

Tyler was so disarmed by her sincerity, that he really opened up. "I spent some time here a couple of summers during college and fell in love with the area. I always wanted to come back. So, here I am. The house really needs work. It is solidly built and is definitely worth the effort."

Barbara said, "Well, in that case, you'll need a good contractor."

"Do you know of any?"

In an exasperated voice, Barbara responded, "Do I know any? I told you I know everyone and everything that goes on in this county. I know all of the contractors. However, there is only one that is the best."

"And who would that be?" Tyler asked

"Her name is Serena Milner." Barbara said. "She is by far the *best* in the west, my lifelong *best* friend, and heads and tails the *best* contractor in three counties," emphasizing 'best' every time she said it.

Tyler responded in good fun, "She sounds like the *best*."

"She most definitely is," Barbara continued. "I am sure you saw all of the construction going on around the courthouse."

"I did," Tyler responded.

"Well, Serena is the contractor doing all of the work. She outbid everyone else and will do a quality job. The people here love her."

"Do you think she'd help me?"

"You tell her Barbara sent you and she'll understand," Barbara encouraged. "She's probably out there right now, if you want to talk to her. She will be wearing jeans and work boots, with short, brown hair."

Tyler said, exaggerating, "Thanks, I'll do that, because of your excellent recommendation."

Barbara laughed and responded "Tyler, one more thing. I told you she is my best friend. I love her dearly. You should know she is very attractive and is a lesbian, and does not take kindly to men hitting on her. Just a word of warning. She'll work for you. But if there are any signs of a pass, she'll drop you like a bag of bricks."

Tyler, once again opening up, said "Believe me, Barbara, the last thing I want now is a relationship. I just left one and have no desire for another in the foreseeable future."

CHAPTER TEN

Tyler left the building and looked towards the construction site. There was a ton of activity. Workers were on the roof installing new roof boards and getting prepared to put on new shingles on the hip roof; the kind that would withstand hurricane force winds. Swing stage scaffolding was coming off the side of the building. Workers were repairing the large windows on the courthouse. The concrete sidewalks were upended and, at the same time, workers were removing the old concrete. Some workers were leveling, laying sand, and placing bricks down on the new surface to give the sidewalk more of a colonial look. A new parking lot was being built with colonial style lamp posts and fixtures, all surrounded by brick walls that matched the sidewalks.

The amount of work that was being done outside was impressive; and that was not counting the work that was being done inside.

He saw a woman walking backwards towards a pickup truck in the parking lot, yelling at the men working the concrete as she moved. He knew this had to be Serena Milner. As he approached, he noticed what Barbara had said. She was very, very attractive, in a tomboy way. She was about 5'6" or 5'7" tall, slim and muscular, maybe thirty-one or thirty-two years old. Her brown hair was short and styled in a shag. Her t-shirt was not tight, but it wasn't overly loose either. Her biceps were defined, her breasts were not large, but not small either. They were very well defined. She had on blue jeans and work boots, which gave her a masculine look. But her rear end really was a work of art. It was literally perfect, in Tyler's mind. It is the kind of rear end that men would always give a second glance, which Tyler did immediately.

She stopped and as he got closer, and he heard her yelling at the men, "Goddamn it, Billy, just do your fucking job. I don't have time for this bullshit." Tyler was about ten feet from her and hesitated. From a distance, he heard something coming from the concrete area, but he could only make some jumbled words; he did hear the word "bitch" loud and clear.

Serena shot back, "No, you are a son of a bitch, and a jackass. Just do your fucking job."

Serena turned towards the truck and noticed Tyler standing there. In a menacing tone she said, "Who in the *hell* are you?" with the emphasis on 'hell.'

Tyler raised his hands in surrender and said, "Whoa! Simmer down."

Serena shot back immediately, "Who in the hell are you to tell me to simmer down?"

"My name is Tyler," he stammered. "If you are Serena Milner, your friend Barbara inside said I could find you out here."

And Serena looked directly at Tyler for the first time. Their eyes met and she was immediately disarmed. She had never seen eyes like that before. Tyler had no clue the effect his eyes had on people. He only knew it was a trait that everyone commented on, but he took it for granted. He had just 'pretty eyes,' like some would say. Most people became transfixed for just that initial second. As for Serena, his eyes definitely calmed her.

After a good ten seconds, Serena said questioningly, "I'm sorry. Tyler, is it?"

"Tyler Harrington," he responded.

"I'm sorry, Mr. Harrington," she stated. "This job has been

extraordinarily difficult, not to mention some of the *difficult* people I have to work with. What can I do for you?"

"Call me Tyler. Mr. Harrington was my father. I just purchased a property that is badly in need of renovation and..."

Serena interrupted, "You bought the old Washington place, didn't you?"

"Yes, I did."

"We were all wondering who had bought it, someone up north. A Mr. Johnson from up north purchased it a long time ago and never moved in.

"I know," Tyler said. "Your friend Barbara just gave me the history. And she also gave me your name and how to find you out here. I need a contractor badly. My aim is to do as much as the renovation as possible, more as a job than as a necessity. I need a contractor to help with permitting and with the work I cannot possibly do, like plumbing and HVAC."

"Tyler," Serena responded. "Barbara and I grew up together as best friends and she still is my best friend. I love her dearly. So, I can say this. She has a goddamned big mouth and doesn't know how to filter what comes out of it. She says what's on her goddamn mind when it is on her mind, and sometimes doesn't think of how another may feel. I have three different jobs going right now and this one, by far, has been fucking horrible. Finding good, reliable sons of bitches to work is hard, as well as getting the quality of work that I demand. I cannot possibly take on a new job until well into next year. It's November now. I won't be available until at least February at the earliest. I'm sorry."

Tyler again raised his hands in submission and said, "Thank you for your time." She was about to respond when they heard a big bang and some cussing. Serena looked towards the commotion and yelled, "Billy, what the fuck happened, you jackass?"

Tyler thought, *Colorful, to say the least.* He nodded to her and walked away. As he walked away, Serena felt bad and shook her head. Not one of her better first meetings. She prided herself on her work relationships. Her mantra as a contractor was to be on time when you say you will be somewhere, and always put your customer first, no matter what.

As he walked away, she immediately thought of his eyes—What a look. Then she noticed that he was attractive. He had to be 6'1". Thin, with broad shoulders, with a little bit of a waist, but not much. He had a thin face, pronounced jaw, and a full head of unruly raven black hair, combed back, yet still messy. The two-day growth of beard really made him look good, in a roguish way.

Then she caught herself. It had been so long since she had been in a relationship, she knew it was only a matter of time before she would begin and fail at another. No way. Not going to happen to her again. No way. But those eyes! Wow!

CHAPTER ELEVEN

Edenton is a quiet little town in eastern North Carolina. It was incorporated in 1722, named after a Governor of North Carolina Charles Eden, and was the first capital of North Carolina, from 1722 to 1743[1].

The Chowan County Courthouse is located in the small business district, along with shops, restaurants, and other tourist-y businesses. It is very typical of a small Carolina town with a tight-knit population. Parking in the business district is angled on Broad Street, the main thoroughfare. The waterfront park is located at the end of Broad Street, where summer festivals, concerts, parades, and other events take place over the course of a year.

After the big city life of Philadelphia, this is exactly where Tyler wanted to be. He felt a connection to the area from the time he spent here in college. There was very little night life, which was ok with him. There were no big shopping malls, which was also ok with him. There is a great local hospital, and the town's farmers market was perfect for him to get whatever ingredients he would ever need for cooking. Fixing up the house, and mainly the kitchen, was his goal. He had no idea what he would do with the kitchen once it was completed, but somehow, he knew it was what would help him heal and move forward.

Kathy Gilson, Tyler's publicist, had been calling him non-stop for a week. She had driven from Philadelphia to Edenton to corner him and get him to rethink his choices. Kathy was not only his publicist, but was also a life-long friend. They had gone to high school together, knew each other in passing, but didn't get close until she started dating Jerry Gilson, Tyler's good friend. The last couple of years of high school and some of Tyler's college years they all had spent together. Jerry, a middle manager in a large petroleum firm, had stayed local in Philadelphia after college, and when Tyler moved back to Philadelphia, their friendship had continued. They played racquetball and tennis together, and both had helped Kathy get her business going.

He agreed to meet her at Millie's, the popular watering hole that everyone frequented. It was the only true watering hole in town, which is why everyone frequented it. He walked in around 5:45 PM for a 6:00 PM meeting with Kathy. His eyes adjusted to the lighting and chose a booth near the door for a quick getaway, if need be. He ordered a beer and was lost in thought when Barbara and a friend came in.

She stopped right at his booth and said, "Well, if it isn't the most celebrated chef from Philadelphia, Tyler Harrington himself."

Standing up, Tyler replied conspiratorially, while shaking her hand, "You've been busy on the internet this afternoon. What do your bosses say when you surf the net all day?"

"They know I need my time to gather all of the information stored in this head. Without me they'd be lost," she responded.

"They'd be lost, or you just couldn't live with yourself not knowing everything about everybody," Tyler countered. "I want to thank you for your help today."

Her friend interrupted their banter. "I don't know who this guy is but he sure knows you. Hi, I'm Janice," and extended her hand in greeting. Then she looked into his eyes and was momentarily quiet.

Tyler said, "Hi Janice, I'm Tyler Harrington," shaking her hand.

Janice said, a little besides herself, "My, oh my, but you were right, Barbara. He is a handsome devil. Why, if I wasn't engaged, you'd definitely be on my dance card, especially with *those* eyes!"

Tyler reddened and said "I've got to give it to you, ladies. You definitely make a fellow feel welcome. Very nice to meet you, Janice. I'm sure Barbara will tell you all about me."

Without missing a beat, Barbara said, "Oh, you can be sure of that. Would you like to join us for a libation?"

Tyler said, "As tempting as it is, I must decline. I'm meeting someone here in a few minutes".

"Well," Barbara said, "it has been a pleasure seeing you again, and hope to see you again soon."

"Nice meeting you," Janice added.

Tyler responded, "And you as well."

They left him and took a booth near the bar, probably their favorite booth, which also had a good view of the booth Tyler was sitting in. He knew they would be watching him for the entire duration of his meeting.

A minute later, Kathy walked in and Tyler rose and gave her a big hug. She sat down, he motioned to the bartender, and in a minute a glass of white wine was delivered.

Kathy started, "It is so good to see you in one piece. I was so worried until you returned my call. And, I'm really pissed off at you, as is Jerry. No call, no note, just disappeared. What were you thinking?"

"Come on, Kathy, you know I had to get away. Hell, she put my stuff in storage. Just moved me out," Tyler said emphatically, waving his arms around. She knew he was getting excited and she just sat down. He continued "She doesn't give a rat's ass about me and I'm not sure she ever did."

Kathy said, "Calm down, Tyler. I didn't come here to get you all riled up. In fact, maybe I should. I've never seen you lose your cool and maybe that is what you need, just get it all out. Moving down here came out of nowhere! Are you crazy?"

A little too loud, Tyler said, "Yes, I am crazy!"

Pushing his forearms down with her hands, Kathy said, "Ok. Calm down. I'm sorry." Tyler looked into his beer. Kathy waited for a minute to let him settle down.

During the lull in their conversation, the door opened and Serena Milner walked in. She looked at the booth and saw Tyler talking to a good-looking blonde. She already had looked his way and he looked back, so she nodded her head to him and he nodded back in recognition. Serena was too embarrassed to say hello. She kept walking, work boots, jeans, and all. Tyler couldn't help but watch her as she walked away.

Kathy caught him looking at Serena and said, "Well, I guess you are not hopeless after all."

Tyler said, "Sorry. She's a contractor. I met her today and our meeting was somewhat confrontational, on her part. But she does look great in a pair of jeans."

Kathy looked frustrated, "Well, the bad news is you have had your heart broken. The good news is that everything still works, as in you staring at her butt for a full thirty seconds. All men are pigs."

"Bullshit." Tyler countered. "Women do the exact same thing. And then talk about it later. Men just stare and then go on their way. It's like a rating game that never ends."

"You are a pig. But I still love you!" Kathy responded. "You and Jerry are exactly alike. No wonder you two get along so well."

"I'll call him tomorrow and apologize for you driving all of this way for nothing," Tyler conceded.

"Thank you. He will appreciate it. He feels just as bad about this as I do. What a bitch!"

"I didn't see it coming at all," Tyler said with frustration. "How could I have let the whole thing happen?"

"That is why I am here; you need to hear from someone close to you that none of this was your choice. It was all her choice. You are you. Period."

Tyler said, "But that doesn't change the fact that she and her new boyfriend took my restaurant away from me. I built that place," he raised his voice a little, "and she, her fuck friend and their partners took the place right out from under me. It was my dream, my blood and sweat that built it, and now I'm out. We were together for 6 years, built that business, and then out of nowhere, poof, it's all gone...our life together was what, a lie?"

"People change, Tyler," Kathy said conciliatorily. "Like I said, it was her choice, not yours. And if it is any consolation, she and the rest of the investors are now sitting in an empty restaurant. You were the heart and soul of the place. Once the menu was changed and customers found out you were no longer there, the new chef could not hold a candle to your talent. It went downhill in a matter of a few weeks. They have closed it already."

Tyler said resignedly "Oh, that really makes me feel good. I worked my ass off to build that place and, in a few weeks, it went out. Great. Really makes me feel good!"

"Sarcasm does not become you," Kathy responded. "I liked her and to do to you what she did, blind-sided me also. Everyone in our circle was hurt and felt really, really bad for you. You two were like a married couple in our eyes. Betraying you, she also betrayed our entire circle of friends. And to take away your restaurant right from under your feet was as low as someone could get." After a pause, she continued, "I know this won't sound right, but I have to say it. It's better that it happened now than later, this kind of betrayal. At least here there are no kids involved."

Tyler said, "Oh, that makes me feel better."

"Stop," Kathy said. "You know what I mean. If you don't think I don't get hit on all of the time, think again. Look at me. I'm gorgeous."

They both laughed.

"Seriously," she continued. "Jerry and I talk about this all of the time. From time to time, he has been hit on too. In my case, only the single, rich players hit on me. They know money and cars and stuff is attractive to some women and a married woman is less likely to give up her life, and kids, for a full time relationship. They both want the adventure and challenge. They just want the sex. No fuss, no muss. It is such a betrayal for a married person to engage in that kind of activity. It's so meaningless and demeaning to your partner. It's shallow and unforgivable. I guarantee your ex-girlfriend will be out on the streets. The glamor and romance of owning a restaurant is gone for her boyfriend. It's just a matter of time."

"Well, I'm done with her. I never want to see her again."

"Good for you," Kathy responded. Then she continued, "Ok. Now that's out of the way, let's talk business."

"Kathy, come on. You really can't be serious?" Tyler said.

"Hey," she started. "I made you who you are, at least in the eyes of your fan base. You are not only a good friend, but you are one of my best success stories. I am not going to let you ruin your reputation over your ex-girlfriend. Besides, I'm being selfish when I say I have made a lot of money over your career. Yours is one of the better achievements of my firm. You have been my poster boy for a long time. I'm not going to give that up so easily."

"Kathy," he started.

She interrupted "Don't 'Kathy' me. As your publicist I'm telling you your career is well under way. Tyler, you are not only one of my best friends, but you are also the best chef I have ever been associated with. And you are not even 35 yet. I'm not blowing smoke up your ass. You know it too. No matter where you are or what has happened, your talent will always win over the day. Use it. Don't throw it away over a bad experience. When you burn a piece of chicken, you throw it away and start over with a new piece."

Tyler said, "So now women are just burned pieces of chicken?"

She laughed, "You know what I'm saying. Experiences, not women. Not to say I wouldn't mind burning her ass a little."

"Which brings me to the business part of this meeting," she continued. "I have an associate who retired here in town that I've known forever from the Children Help fundraising days. Remember, you did a couple of those galas for me. Her name is Caroline Jackson. I'm going to meet with her tonight before I head back. We... are going to meet with her tonight. When she found out you moved here, she was beside herself. She has a party every year the Saturday after Thanksgiving for the local Children Fund."

"Oh, come on, Kathy," Tyler said for a second time.

"Stop the 'Come On, Kathy' bit. This is for your mental health and you know it will put you back into the right state of mind. You love it. Go for it. Impress yourself as well as the people who will be attending. This is you, Tyler. Admit it. I'm here to start to give you your life back." She added a little sheepishly, "And, I still need to impress Caroline with you. I need her support, or I should say her husband's company business."

"Kathy," Tyler said resignedly, "you are a piece of work. That is why I love you so dearly."

"Now we have to go. We've been here long enough. We have to meet Caroline. Next time Jerry and the kids will come with me and we'll spend the weekend. And by the way, those three women over there have been looking our way the entire time we have been talking."

Tyler said, "I know. The one in the middle is Barbara, the local busy-body. She helped me today in the county office. I bought an old house and will be remodeling it for the foreseeable future. That is going to be my therapy. The one on the left is Janice. She's nice, and I take it, a little ditzy. The one on the right is Serena, a local contractor and a lesbian. The one with the nice body is a lesbian. Just my luck. No matter; I think I'm going to like this town. Way different than Philly."

"My word," Kathy said, "All of that in less than twenty-four hours. I can't believe you bought a house."

"I did," he replied," and wait until you see it. It's an old Georgian on a bluff overlooking the river. I didn't know there were any bluffs in this area, but there is one that the house sits on. When I'm done, it will really be something."

Tyler went up to the bar and paid his tab, introducing himself to Todd, the bartender. He came back to the booth, helped Kathy on with her very nice overcoat, and on the way out turned, smiled, and gave a two-finger, forehead hand salute to the three ladies who were watching his every move.

Barbara looked down immediately, Serena blushed a beet-red, but Janice waved back. As he was leaving, he heard Barbara say, "Janice," and Janice responded a little too loudly, "but he waved goodbye."

Chapter Twelve

B
arbara and Janice sat in their booth and Todd the bartender
brought them two beers. Immediately Janice started on
Barbara.

"That guy is gorgeous," Janice started. "Who is he?"

Barbara said, "Hold on." Just then, a beautiful blonde walked into the bar, saw Tyler, and gave him a big, big hug.

"Oh, my word", Barbara whispered, as they watched the interaction between Tyler and his lady friend.

Janice said, "Come on, Barbara. What do you know?"

Barbara started by saying "Well, what I found out today..." but cut herself off when Tyler raised his voice and was waving his hands in the air.

Janice watched too, and when he calmed down, turned to Barbara and said, "This is very interesting."

As Serena came in, Barbara said, "Now it's going to get interesting."

They saw Serena nod to Tyler and Tyler nod back, and watched Tyler's eyes follow Serena all of the way to the booth. Todd brought over Serena a glass of white wine and said hello.

Serena looked at Barbara and said, "Don't start on me."

Barbara said, "Hey, you were the butthole today, not me. I got you introduced not only to potential business, but also the best looking guy this town has seen in a long time."

Serena sounded apologetic, "I feel terrible. You guys know I'm not usually like that, especially to someone looking to hire me. But your boyfriend Billy," she accusingly looked at Janice, "once again pissed me off so bad, I lost my temper."

Janice said sheepishly, "You know he likes you, Serena. He just likes to get your goat every now and then."

Serena reacted, "Get my goat? That's different than just pissing me off. And he called me a bitch today."

"Well, you are a bitch." They all three laughed.

"So, who's the blonde?" Serena asked. "I was going to apologize to him but thought better of it."

"I've been trying to get information from Barbara but she is too busy watching them," complained Janice.

"Come on, Barbara. Out with it."

"Well," she started, "his name is Tyler Harrington."

Serena interrupted "We know that. Cut to the chase."

"As I was saying," Barbara continued patiently. "His name is Tyler Harrington and he is a chef from Philadelphia; a famous chef in that city and on the entire east coast. He built and opened a restaurant in downtown Philadelphia and it became the toast of the town; very, very successful. People from all over the world visiting Philadelphia had trouble getting reservations there. His live-in girl-friend of six years, according to the article, was an investor in the business along with several other people. She, and the other investors, forced him out when he wouldn't expand the way they wanted him to. I read in another article that his ex-girlfriend and one of the investors bought him out, and that they were an item. They became the new managing partners of the business."

"Wow," Janice and Serena said at the same time.

Barbara continued, "Within two months, again, according to the article, when people found out Tyler was no longer there, the restaurant failed. They brought in a celebrated chef from New York, but the place was known as Tyler's place and it went under quickly."

Serena was in awe, "Barbara, you are unbelievable. How you get so much information so quickly is beyond me."

Barbara seemed proud of her accomplishment. "Admit it. That is why you love me."

"You were that way when we were growing up, in high school, and still are now," Serena responded.

"It's a gift."

Janice interrupted them. "Look how animated he is. Do you think he'll hit her?"

"Don't be stupid," Barbara said.

"I bet that is the girlfriend who dumped him," Janice continued.

Barbara interjected "No way. He would probably have hit her already if that was her. At least I know my Craig would knock me out and then leave. He is such a Neanderthal."

"That guy is not a Neanderthal." Serena said, as she continued to watch Tyler and the blonde. "Look at him. He is composed, yet passionate. He picks his words and gestures to emphasize them. His expression is pleasant all of the time; yet again, his expressions show his meaning and intent. His eyes are transfixing. I don't know how that lady is talking to him without looking into his eyes and melting." Serena was looking at Tyler and felt the silence. She looked over at her friends, "What?"

Both Barbara and Janice looked at Serena with mouths open.

Barbara, of course, said "Oh my Lanta. You are in love."

"What? No, I'm not," Serena defended herself.

Janice added, "Oh yes, you are. Look at you, the way you are looking at him. I bet you have already undressed him in your mind."

Barbara joined in the ribbing, "I guess we are going to have to dispel the lesbian rumor, finally. That was so stupid to begin with."

Serena shot back in more of a whisper, "Don't you dare. I cannot take those guys anymore. Just leave it be."

Barbara added, "Your choice. But admit it. You like him, don't you?"

"I don't know him," She whispered again. "I just feel bad that I was such a bitch to him today. It was totally uncalled for and not who I am."

Their conversation drifted back and forth and suddenly Tyler was up and moving to the bar. All three women watched his every move.

As he left with the blonde, he turned and saluted them. Barbara looked down immediately, Serena blushed, but Janice waved back.

Barbara said, "Janice."

And Janice said a little too loudly, "But he waved goodbye."

After he was gone, they all three started to giggle. Then Todd came to the table and set a beer down in front of Janice and said, "This is from the gentleman named Tyler that just left."

He set a second beer in front of Barbara, and then a third beer in front of Serena, along with a shot of tequila.

Todd said, "Tyler told me to tell potty mouth that 'he hopes the shot will simmer her down a little.' His words, Serena, not mine," as he held the tray in front of him like a shield.

They all busted out laughing and Barbara said, "I think he likes you, Serena."

Serena said "Don't be so high-school, Barbara. It's just a drink. And, I was a little nasty to him today."

"I'd say," Barbara added, "You must have cussed up a storm to get a shot of tequila, potty mouth."

Just then, Billy walked in and slid down next to Janice. Serena said, "You are a jackass, Billy," to which he replied, "And you are a bitch, Serena."

Janice rushed to stop them, "Okay, now that is out of the way, can we please enjoy our drinks?"

"Honey, I can only stay for a drink," he announced. I have to go to Mrs. Jackson's house to get my marching orders for the fundraiser. She's having a short meeting tonight for everyone involved."

Immediately, Serena chimed in, "Even though I hate you, Billy, whatever help you need let me know. I've got tents and chairs and tables if they are needed. And, whatever construction material you need, I'll provide. And, the guys will all help, you know that.

"You are a bitch, Serena, but a good bitch. Just like the one in the bubble in the Wizard of Oz," Billy said, amused by his own humor.

Janice interrupted their banter and asked Barbara, "Have you gotten a gown for it yet?"

"No. We may have to go to Raleigh to find one, one that shows these puppies off," Barbara pointed to her breasts.

Caroline Jackson's annual Thanksgiving fundraiser was one of the town's most anticipated events for the resident townspeople. It was not part of the tourist scene and was a great time for everyone to get together after the holiday. People dressed in gowns and jackets and it was truly a gilded soiree. Mrs. Jackson's home was one of the largest in town and had a small ballroom, living area, and yard space to accommodate a crowd. She would have food tables under tents and several bars throughout the house and yard. It was all for a good cause and most attendees donated generously.

Their talk drifted back and forth for a while and Tyler was forgotten.

CHAPTER THIRTEEN

After his meeting with Kathy and Mrs. Jackson, he had returned home just as the cleaning crew was leaving the house for the day. As he got back to the hotel, he realized it had been a long day and a lot had happened in just a quick twelve hours.

The next day, he arrived at the house early and started the outside trim work that he had planned. It was cold out and the brush wouldn't come out easy. The cleaning crew arrived and started their work.

Late that afternoon, he walked through the house with the supervisor and was amazed at the job they had done. Her name was Maria and if she told Tyler once, she told him six times how she loved the house. Her impression was the same as his—solidly built with craftsmanship that was a lost art in today's houses. The floors, fixtures, mantles, all of the woodwork, was second to none. She did say that the house needed a ton of work, but done properly, it could be a showpiece.

"Mr. Harrington," Maria said, "I have cleaned a lot of houses during my career in this business. None have been as hard as this one. However, watching this house come back into its own has been a true pleasure."

"Thanks," Tyler said. "I appreciate the thought."

"Just so you know," Maria continued. "We all took a turn at trying to clean that bathtub. It refused to come clean. It's clean, but the stains will not come out. You'll probably have to replace it."

"Maria," Tyler added "I plan on replacing all of the fixtures and enlarging and changing the bathrooms."

"That downstairs bathroom is small, isn't it?" She replied.

"You mean the water closet?" Tyler responded.

"Exactly."

After she left, Tyler walked the house and couldn't get over how good it looked. The floors were amazing and would look even better once he sanded and polished the wood. The cleaning crew had done a fabulous job on all of the woodwork. The doors were cleaned but peeling, as were the walls. Much work was still needed inside. He went through his to-do list by order of importance and changed a couple of things.

The next day, the moving truck came. In his mother's house outside of Philadelphia and later on, in his apartment downtown Philadelphia, the furniture had looked overbearing in smaller spaces. In this house, it didn't even make a dent in the space. The house looked empty even after all of the furniture was in. There was a kitchen table set, a living room couch and armchair, a coffee table, two end tables with lamps, and two bedroom sets that were upstairs, including beds, nightstands, dressers, and his mother's vanity, which he cherished. Many hours were spent in her room while she sat in front of that vanity talking; memories that would be with him forever.

He went back to the hotel that evening. That would be his last night there since he had already paid for it. The next day, he would start outside of the house and see what happened. He still needed several additional items from the hardware store, so he decided to go shopping before going back to the hotel. He had to purchase items he had never used in the past. While walking up one aisle of the store, he saw Serena Milner at the counter, talking and purchasing something from the clerk. His stomach jumped and he started sweating. He stopped in his tracks and felt like he was back in middle school. He didn't shy away from a chance meeting, but she was gone in a flash. He felt like running after her just to talk, but that would have been awkward. Why did this woman make him feel like this? He didn't want a relationship; but there was something about her that intrigued him.

After checking out of the hotel, he realized he needed a couple of things from the grocery store, one of which was wine. He wanted to have some around, not that he necessarily drank alone. He really liked wine as a social drink; he always enjoyed it more with someone else.

Serena Milner was driving down the street when she saw Tyler loading groceries into the back of his truck. She instinctively lowered herself in her seat. Then she caught herself. What was that all about? He was just a guy. But she still felt so bad about their first encounter that she really didn't want to just wave as though they were friends. And he made her feel different, not like the usual guys she had been with. There was an attraction she couldn't rationalize or explain away. So, she looked ahead and drove right by. She knew Tyler hadn't noticed her and once again, guilt made her feel very uneasy.

Once at the house, Tyler made up the bedrooms, furnished the bathrooms with towels and necessities, and started emptying kitchen boxes, and other odds and ends. At least, his ex, or whomever she had hired to do it, had been good at packing his things. Very little was broken or damaged, and all of his cooking tools and implements were there—His knives, which always kept with him in his truck, along with his metal detecting equipment. Other than cooking, which was his livelihood, he enjoyed metal-detecting woods, beaches, and other barren areas. This passion was what had brought him to this area when he was in college, a suggestion from his father.

Satisfied, he set his schedule because of the fundraiser, and laid out his plans. He worked in the yard for a while that afternoon, and the next morning. After that little bit of work, he concentrated on the fundraiser. It was only five days away. He knew he would be spending Thanksgiving alone for the first time in his life. He had always cooked to perfection Thanksgiving Day. He loved the holiday, mainly because his restaurants were closed, for his employees' sake, and because he always got to cook for his family and friends.

He would spend the day on the menu for the fundraiser and really knock their socks off. He checked his email that morning and saw that Mrs. Jackson had hired several of the students from the High School culinary program to help him. He sent emails to them and asked them to meet him Friday morning at 8AM at the farmers market to buy fresh produce and start the cooking process.

He was excited. It had been six or seven months since he had done any cooking and being back in a kitchen was what he longed for. He'd have to remember to give Kathy a big kiss for this event. She really was a special person in his life.

Chapter Fourteen

T he day of the gala finally came. Tyler had been extremely busy, so busy that he had forgotten his past pain and had thrown himself entirely into the preparations for the party.

North Carolina leads the nation in sweet potato growing. It produces close to 2 billion pounds of sweet potatoes and is responsible for 50%-60% of sweet potatoes produced in the US annually.[1] After discussing his menu with Mrs. Jackson, she was thrilled with what he wanted to do.

That evening, as the guests arrived, Tyler was busy with his apprentices, making last-minute preparations. He was not able to see what the crowd was like or what kind of mood they were in. He always liked to mingle a little just to get a sense of his audience.

Mrs. Jackson herded all of the guests onto her lawn. It was a beautiful November evening. With a temperature in the mid-sixties, she couldn't have asked for a better evening of weather. On the dais was a microphone and Mrs. Jackson started by saying "May I have your attention please! I am thrilled that all of you came out this evening. And before all else, you have my heartfelt gratitude for the generous donations of time and money to the Children Fund. I thank you all from the bottom of my heart."

A big round of applause was in progress as Tyler exited the house onto the back of the lawn. He saw Mrs. Jackson in the front speaking and waited for his introduction. He caught sight of Barbara in the front and immediately wondered if Serena would be attending. Why did he think that? Why had that popped into his mind? Why did that spitfire have him thinking about her?

"And now, I'd like to introduce the guest chef for the evening, who recently moved into our area from Philadelphia. This gentleman has been reviewed in the Philadelphia Enquirer, the New York Times, and The Washington Post. He recently was awarded..."

Tyler couldn't listen to it. For as much as he liked his profession, the glitz and glamor was no longer a part of who he was. He knew that now. The next step was to figure out what he would do with his God-given talent and how to move on to the next chapter of his life.

"Ladies and Gentlemen, Mr. Tyler Harrington," she concluded.

Tyler took the dais and the microphone. "Good evening. I am Tyler Harrington and do we ever have a treat for everyone tonight. I want to first thank Mrs. Jackson for this wonderful event and for inviting me to participate. I have been part of the Children Fund for over 5 years now and each event is different and fun to attend. In the past, it was always a treat to not only participate, but more importantly, to know the good we all do for the kids. That's what this is all about."

He went on, "Since it is only two days since your thanksgiving feast, tonight will *not* be about filling up. It will be about *aroma*, *taste*, and *texture*," as he emphasized the three words. "I'd like to introduce Ellie, Henry, Josh, and Josie from the high school culinary program. These young adults did all of the cooking. Trust me. They did the work and afterwards will answer any of your questions about the food you're about to sample."

All four young chefs stood next to Tyler in their clean smocks and white hats. Tyler, of course, had his blacks on, with his name embossed in red across his chest pocket.

"We all know about sweet potatoes. You just had candied sweet potatoes two days ago, along with sweet potato pie for dessert, right?" he queried the crowd, always wanting to get everyone involved with the show. A nod of heads and a consensual murmur rose.

"Sweet potatoes are the state vegetable and North Carolina produces almost 60% of the sweet potatoes in the country, all coming from this area of the state. Everyone is proud to be a part of the sweet potato industry. But let me ask you all. How many of you have ever experienced sweet potatoes other than what you make on Thanksgiving? The idea tonight is not to eat a lot. It is to go into the house, into the big room, and smell first. Let your sense of smell guide you. Each of the 30 items that have been prepared are different, and they all are made with sweet potatoes. I promise you, you will be amazed at what you sample. It's about taste and texture. Each dish has a name card describing what it is and the ingredients used, along with small wooden spoons to sample. Sorry, no calorie counts here. I'm afraid I'd get run out of town by those who watch calories. But there are at least 10 dishes that are vegan and are marked as such. Please try them all."

He continued "Mrs. Jackson also requested some BBQ and iced shrimp for those who do not have a taste for sweet potatoes, along with some salads. Please enjoy yourselves. Before we begin, are there any questions?"

A gentleman in the middle asked, "Are there any desserts?"

"Oh, I'm sorry." Tyler responded "I failed to mention it. We have prepared five different desserts, all made with sweet potatoes, of course. We made more of the desserts for those of you with a terrible sweet tooth."

Everyone laughed. Someone yelled out "You are from Philly. What do you know about sweet potatoes?"

Without missing a beat, Tyler responded "I yam what I yam!"

A big groan came from the crowd.

Tyler said, "*Y'all* knew I had to say that eventually," which got a big laugh and a round of applause.

"Thank you, and please enjoy the evening."

Mrs. Jackson grabbed the microphone and yelled "How about a

big round of applause for our chefs!" to which the crowd responded enthusiastically.

Inside, the guests were bowled over by the setting. There were three large, long tables in different parts of the ballroom, another table in the dining room, and one table in the living room. All of the tables had white table clothes and were filled with the different recipe dishes. Each dish was accompanied by a bowl of small wooden spoons, like you get in school with ice cream, and a place card in front of each dish describing what it was and the ingredients used.

There were roasted garlic slices, mashed sweet potato in pate choux, 7-layer slices with bechamel and thyme, fritters, stuffed, smoked and on and on. It was impressive. The guests loved it, as if they were in an extravagant tasting. With each taste, they would remark on the flavors, herbs and seasoning, comparing the dish to some exotic item they had in the orient or middle east. Each dish was an experience. That is how Tyler knew they were enjoying it. The wine, which was flowing generously, didn't hurt either.

Towards the end of the sampling, when most guests were outside, Tyler was behind the table in the dining room near the kitchen looking at his phone, when Serena walked up to him. She said, "Hello Tyler." He looked up and was startled. She had a gown on that was simply incredible. She was beautiful.

After several numb, silent seconds, he held his hands over his private parts and said, "Good to see you attended, Miss Milner."

She laughed and said "No worries. I don't have my work boots on. And, it's Serena."

"Well, Serena. Without sounding too impertinent, you look absolutely fabulous. And please, take that as a compliment."

"I do. And likewise, you have really outdone yourself and this town tonight. They will be talking about this event for weeks to come, let alone never having candied yams again," she said laughing.

Just then, the four students approached him and started jabbering all at once. They couldn't express their appreciation to him enough. Serena started to walk away and he interrupted the students and said "Serena, would you join me in a couple of minutes for a glass of wine. I'm parched." She said "Sure. I'll be right outside."

"Whoa, Mr. Tyler," Josh said, "You do know..." Tyler interrupted him. "Yes Josh. Leave it be."

They went on to thank him for the experience and all asked him to please come into their class and talk to everyone else in the program. Their teacher was there and couldn't believe the work they did. It really was special for them. Tyler agreed that he would come to the school and speak.

Then he said, "And what did you also learn in your classes?"

Ellie spoke up first. "That we have to clean the kitchen when we are done."

"That's right," Tyler said smiling. "When you are a chef your proteges do the clean-up."

Henry chimed in "That just ain't right, Mr. T. My hands can't take much more scrubbing."

"The good news is that most of the big cleaning is done. You all have done a bunch and I've already done a lot of it while you all were mingling. That is why we clean as we go. I just don't want to leave Mrs. Jackson's kitchen in a mess. Now chop-chop, and come and get me when you are done so I can inspect your work." he said smiling.

They went into the kitchen chatting away about the responses on the different menu items. He loved these young students and what they did. Visiting their class might be a good thing for him.

CHAPTER FIFTEEN

T yler grabbed a glass of wine, went out to the lawn and found Serena talking with an elderly couple. Tyler approached them and was immediately accosted by the couple. They thanked him profusely, chatted for a minute, and then made their way to another group of friends.

Serena said, "I didn't think you'd come out."

Tyler said "Please don't think I take our first meeting personally. You were having a bad day and I get it. I've had plenty of those in the last couple of months. I do think the shot of tequila was a nice touch, don't you?"

She replied "Yes it was. Not so sure about the potty mouth bit. Barbara and Janice have been calling me that all week."

Tyler said "Sorry. But you do have a potty mouth."

She said "I know. It comes with trade, so to speak. My father was in the business and both of my brothers are still in the business, one in Charlotte and the other is in Atlanta. I grew up learning English in High School and on the job-sites learned another language altogether."

They both laughed.

A middle aged African American couple approached them and Serena said "Tyler, I'd like you to meet Sandra and Charlie."

They were both in their mid-sixties, healthy, slim, both attractive in their evening attire. Sandra had shoulder length hair, a round face, and deep brown eyes. Charlie had a weathered look; short graying hair, huge, calloused hands, and his countenance had a continuous, genial look.

Sandra said, "Very pleased to meet you, Tyler. We enjoyed your presentation."

Charlie blurted "The only person I know that can do as much with a sweet potato as you did is my Auntie Pia."

Serena chimed in "And that is a huge compliment, Tyler. Auntie Pia is a gem. Charlie and my father were in the construction business together for years. They worked together from here to Raleigh and to Durham. I worked with both of them growing up."

Charlie said, "I taught this young lady everything she knows about construction."

Serena interrupted "You are full of shit Charlie".

Charlie finished by saying "But I didn't teach her everything I know. HehHeh."

Sandra admonished him "Charlie Washington, you know this girl has done her bit on her own. She now runs circles around you."

Serena added "Charlie is semi-retired."

And Sandra added "The only reason he still does some work is to get him out of the house and out of my hair. Just looking for some peace and quiet."

Tyler came out of his thoughts and said "Washington? Is that your last name?"

And Charlie said "My whole life, and most of hers," pointing to Sandra.

Then Sandra figured it out. "You bought the old homestead, didn't you?"

"Yes Ma'am, he responded. I've been told it is still known as the Washington House."

Charlie said "No offense, but it probably always will be. My family owned that house for over 125 years. Then my great uncle got into some trouble and he had to sell it. I'm sure you'll do right by it."

Just then Barbara, Craig, Janice, and Billy all came up to their group and Barbara said "Charlie, do you *ever* stop talking."

Sandra chimed in "No he doesn't Barbara."

Charlie responded "Tyler, most people use the internet. Around here, we use inter-Barbara."

Sandra grabbed Charlie by the arm and started pulling him away. They said their goodbyes and were gone. Billy and Craig went to get everyone more wine.

Barbara started, "Ok, Mr. Chef. Spill the beans. Who was the blonde?"

Janice and Serena both exclaimed at the same time "Barbara!"

Tyler laughed. He really liked this group of people. Down deep he wanted them to like him too. They were all refreshingly genuine, not what he was used to.

Tyler teased "She is beautiful, isn't she?"

They all nodded.

"Her name is Kathy. She and her *husband* Jerry and their 2 kids are my closest friends. And, she is also my publicist."

Barbara said "Ooh, a publicist."

Tyler continued," Kathy is the person who made this happen tonight with her connection to Mrs. Jackson. I sort of disappeared for a couple of months and when she finally tracked me down, she came here to check up on me and to express her displeasure with me."

Craig and Billy came back with the drinks and Billy said "Serena, that dress..." and before he could finish Barbara and Janice, both pushed him back and away from the group at the same time. Craig said "I better rescue Billy. It was really nice meeting you Tyler."

Tyler said "Craig, I promised Barbara I'd comment..."

"I know", he interrupted. "She does that all of the time. If it makes her happy, it makes me happy."

All three at the same time said, "A happy wife is a happy life," and all laughed out loud.

Craig left and Serena said "I've got a business proposition for you. Charlie is driving Sandra crazy at home. She needs to get him out of the house. If he agrees, Charlie can work for you and I'll pull all of the permits and get my contacts to schedule work. You pay all of them directly since I really won't be doing any of the work. You pay Charlie, sort of as your contractor, and he will keep all of the plumbers and electricians in line. He is slowing down but can still manage the job. I'll just charge you for any time I spend doing whatever.

Wide-eyed, Tyler said without hesitating "Deal! My word, you are a godsend."

She said "Not so fast. He will literally talk your ear off. All you have to say to him is to give it a rest for a while and he'll get the message. Charlie and I will come by Monday morning around 7AM to formally set it up. I think he'll be excited to work on his old homestead and Sandra will be just as happy!"

Chapter Sixteen

On Monday morning Serena and Charlie both drove up to the house. Tyler was just finishing getting dressed and met them at the front door.

Charlie whistled and shook his head saying "Lordy, Lordy! I haven't been here in 30 years. This place needs a ton of work." Serena was looking around and shaking her head too.

Tyler said "The inside was just as bad as the outside. Come in and take a look because the cleaning crew finished it."

They all went in and Charlie said "I might get a little choked up. This is just how I remember it. Man, the memories here. Did Maria do this work?"

Tyler said, "Yes, she did a great job."

Serena added "She does do good work. I use her people all the time."

They walked through the house and into the kitchen. Tyler said "This is where I'll make my mark on this house. I have a lot of plans for this kitchen. It is great. I love it."

Serena said "I have a 7:30 meeting. Have to go. You and Charlie work out any details. I've already explained to Charlie our deal and he is on board."

They said their goodbyes and Serena walked through the hall

and out the door, in her jeans and work boots. Tyler watched her go the entire way out the door.

Charlie caught him looking and asked, "What you looking at?"

Tyler decided not to pull any punches with Charlie. "I'm watching a work of art walk through my hallway. What a rear end!"

Charlie said "You watch yourself, Michelangelo. She is like a daughter to me, one of my own. She is just as beautiful on the inside as she is on the outside. A real gem. She has a heart of gold, that one."

Tyler responded "No disrespect intended, Charlie. She came through for me in a big way by setting this up. I'll try my best to repay her kindness."

"You do that," he said, and continued, "It's too bad she was treated the way she was by those men. Twice she had her heart broken and I was there to see it both times, and helped her pick up the pieces."

"By men?" Tyler asked.

"Don't you believe that bullshit Barbara spread. Those construction guys were hitting on her like there was no tomorrow. They came up with that cockamamie lesbian rumor to keep men at bay. She's a good girl and deserves to have a good man someday."

"Now," he continued, "I need to ask you a serious question."

"Fire away," Tyler responded.

"This old house is way outdated." Charlie began. "Just walking in, I noticed it needs a front porch, a new roof, all new wiring, new plumbing, fixtures, and not to exclude what we can't see on the surface, like foundation and septic issues. Do you have enough funds to sink into this place? I mean whatever your budget is in your head, triple it."

"First and foremost," Tyler answered, "this will be my home. I have no plans of fixing it up and then selling. It is not a financial investment; it is a life investment. I want to fix it up the right way, no cutting corners."

Charlie offered, "That's good to hear."

Tyler continued "My parents passed away in a car crash four

years ago. I sold their house and took the proceeds and their insurance money and invested in my restaurant in Philadelphia. When I was forced out, I was paid what I invested plus appreciation from the ongoing business. I do not have unlimited funds. But I think I have enough to cover this project. I'll make it happen, even if I have to work the rest of my life. For some reason I have a connection here, in the south, in this town. I'm here to stay."

"You got it, Tyler." Charlie said. "I'll be watching you with my girl Serena, you can bet on it. Let's do this. One more thing! Rule number 1. What happens here and what's said here, stays here. You run your mouth to Sandra and we'll go to blows. Got it?"

Tyler laughed and said "Deal," shaking his hand.

After that, Charlie took command. He basically scrapped Tyler's to-do list and came up with his own. Charlie might have been in his sixties, but he worked like he was in forties. And he definitely knew how to let subcontractors know what he needed and how he wanted it done. Tyler couldn't have been more fortunate to have someone of his experience and caliber working on his house.

After three weeks of hard work, the outside grounds started to look much better. Because of permitting and other delays, some work had to be postponed or halted until after the holidays. But the house was really starting to shape up.

Tyler's phone buzzed one evening; it was Barbara calling. He said, "How did you get my number?" She responded "Really. This is me you're dealing with. Every Friday we all meet at Millie's around 6PM for a drink. We'd love it if you would join us tomorrow night."

Tyler said "I'd love to. Thank you for the invite. See you there."

Chapter Seventeen

The next evening, after a hard day of work, Tyler and Charlie were sitting on the back stoop. Tyler had brought them a glass of wine and they were just chatting.

Tyler said, "I hope you like this wine, Charlie. I picked up a couple of bottles at the store just to have some here."

Charlie said "Tyler, I never had a bad glass of wine. Some are better than others, but never a *bad* glass."

Tyler laughed. "Charlie, there is no way I'll ever be able to thank you enough for what you have done here already. A whole new roof, with one new beam I may add, and the attic completely finished off, ready for heat and AC. You are a miracle worker in my book. Like I said, I'll never know how to thank you enough."

Charlie said, "Money always helps."

They both laughed for a minute, sipped some wine, and relaxed. Tyler interrupted their meditation by saying "There is something drawing me here and I cannot put my finger on it. I spent a summer in this area while in college at the suggestion of my grandmother. I don't know why, except she said that long ago we had roots here. I want to fit in. And I think some folks here like me. I was invited to Millie's on Friday for drinks with Barbara and her crew. I really like them all."

Charlie said "Especially Serena. Admit it. You got it for that girl. You only ask about her *bidness* every day so you can find out about her."

Tyler smiled and said, "Strictly *bidness*," emphasizing the southern colloquialism.

"Bull shit, you liar," Charlie shot back. "I'm telling you, you had better step slowly with her. I'm serious. She may cuss and have a temper, but she is all woman inside. You need to give her all the space she needs. Believe me, that is 45 years of marriage talking."

Tyler responded, "coming from a man who is the king of his castle, right?"

"Sandra may want to wear the pants of the family, but she knows she needs a good belt to hold them up." Charlie philosophized.

Tyler laughed, "Not really what a feminist, or Sandra for that matter, would want to hear."

Charlie said, "Tyler, when you get to my age, we don't want conflict, we don't want confrontation. But if I happen to say something that insults someone, I will apologize and try my best to not do it again. I don't want to intentionally hurt people. I don't think anyone does. But damn it, sticks and stones, you know. There is a famous quote from Thomas Jefferson where he said, and I don't remember the exact quote, 'it is none of my business if it does not pick my pocket or break my leg'. Live and let live."

Tyler said, "You're a smart man, Charlie Washington."

Charlie continued "I know what we need to do. Tomorrow is Thursday and a light day. Those electricians won't be here until Monday and the plumbers can't start until the electricians are done. Let's knock off early and go see Aunt Pia. When I stop there on my way home tonight, I'll let her know we'll be visiting tomorrow afternoon."

Tyler said, "What is it you think she'll tell us?"

Charlie said "Who knows. She is 94 or 95 years old and ornery as a polecat. She says she was born in 1925 but cannot prove it. Really pisses her off when we bring the subject up. Anyway, her body is failing like any other 95 year old. But, I have *never, ever* met anyone of her age with a mind or memory as sharp as hers. She still lives alone in the house she has had since after WW2, and has some issues getting around. But Sandra loves her just as much as I do and we take care of her. We are over there every day. Sandra watches her 'stories' with her, those stupid soaps in the afternoon."

"Do you think she would know if I had any connections here?" Tyler asked.

"There is only one way to find out. We'll go tomorrow," Charlie answered.

CHAPTER EIGHTEEN

The next day, they drove to Aunt Pia's house. It was a small 1950's style one-level ranch house, very well kept and up to date on the outside. After going in, Tyler noticed the inside was just as current and well kept. He could tell Charlie and Sandra spent a lot of time there.

After knocking on the door and yelling, they went in. Aunt Pia was sitting in her chair in the small living room with the TV on, her walker right next to her chair. They went in and Charlie gave her a kiss on the cheek and said,

"How you doing today, Aunt Pia?"

She said "Just fine and dandy, boy. How have you been?"

Charlie said "Aunt Pia, I like you to meet Tyler Harrington. He is the fellow I've been working with at the old house."

Tyler said, "It is very nice to meet you, Mrs. Washington."

She looked up and said "Oh call me Aunt Pia. Everyone calls me . . ." And she stopped mid-sentence when she looked into Tyler's eye's.

Charlie said "What is it, Aunt Pia? You ok?"

It took her a good seven to eight seconds of staring at Tyler to find her voice. Then she blurted out, pointing at Tyler "You are a *Thorne*. I know those eyes. You are a Thorne."

Charlie said "No, Aunt Pia. This is Tyler Harrington, the young man who bought the old house. He is from Philadelphia."

"I know where he came from without even asking." She gathered herself and said "I'm sorry. Please sit down. You say your name is Harrington?"

Tyler responded, somewhat taken aback, "Yes Ma'am."

"What was our mother's maiden name?"

He answered "Johnson."

"So, your Daddy was a Harrington. What was his mother's maiden name, your grandmother?"

He was stunned. "Her maiden name was Thorne."

Aunt Pia slapped her knee and said "I told you. You are a Thorne."

Charlie said "That is incredible. How did you know that, Aunt Pia?"

"Boy, how many times do I have to tell you that I am old, I am highly educated, a master's degree no less, and you will have to get up way before dawn to outsmart me. You just will never get it, will you?"

"Aunt Pia, stop calling me boy. I am a grown-ass man and I have grandchildren. Why do you have to always call me 'boy'? Lordy, you test me!"

She responded, a little loudly, "I was there the day you were born; I watched your mother nurse you; I changed your diapers; and, I was the one to let you go the first steps you took to your mamma. If anyone has the right to call you 'boy', it's me."

Charlie said, "That just ain't right."

"Why don't you stop talking and go to the kitchen and bring us that iced tea and some of those sweet potato fritters I made."

She looked at Tyler and said,

"Charlie told me you made a whole bunch of stuff with sweet potatoes and the fritters were just as good as mine. He said *I met my match*," mimicking Charlie. "He got me fired up on purpose just so I'd make some. Well, that's a load of bull. I want you to taste my fritters and you be honest with me and tell me the difference."

Tyler couldn't help but laugh.

"Aunt Pia, I can see that the fruit doesn't fall far from the tree."

She cackled, and just as quickly her expression changed, turned to Charlie and said, "Go on boy, go to the kitchen, *please*???"

Tyler knew there was a bond here; a love that he knew from his own parents, and one that really never got to blossom, due to their untimely deaths.

Aunt Pia went on as Charlie went into the kitchen.

"That boy came out of his momma kicking and screaming and he hasn't shut up since. He even talks in his sleep. I have no idea how he can go on and on all the time. Sandra is a saint."

Charlie answered from the kitchen, "Sandra doesn't know how lucky she is to have me."

She rolled her eyes and started.

"The Thorne family goes back 5 generations, 4 generations from Charlie for the Washington family. The way I know it is as it was related to me way back when. Let's see, my grandfather told it to me. Going back 4 generations, your great, great, great, great grandfather was named Ebenezer Thorne. We'll call him g4. He owned a huge plantation on this side of the river from Edenton and grew, of course, sweet potatoes. He had a son named Virgil, your g3. Are you following what I'm saying?"

"Yes Ma'am. Great, great, great, grandfather, g3" Tyler replied.

Charlie came in with the tea and sweet potato fritters on a tray. Aunt Pia said "You like how I did that, Charlie? G3 and g4. That's why I'm the smart one in the family. The internet is not the only thing that uses acronyms."

Charlie replied, "Oh, you are smart alright," very sarcastically.

"Anyway," she continued. "Your g3 grew up and was best friends with my..." paused as she looked up to the ceiling," my g1, my great grandfather Zachariah, or as he was called, Zack. Zack and Virgil were raised together and were just like brothers. Now, this is all coming from my grandfather who told me all of these stories, a true oral history. I just thank the lord I am able to remember them and pass them down to Charlie and his kids. Your g3 was married to a woman from Philadelphia named Phoebe. She moved here and built the house you just bought, with her husband Virgil."

Charlie interrupted, "Aunt Pia, our family lived in that house, not the Thornes."

She snapped at him, "Who is telling this story, Charlie Washington? Don't you interrupt me. It is a long story and very complicated, to say the least!"

"Yes Ma'am," Charlie answered.

She began again, "Charlie, go up into the attic and bring me down that tomato box, the one with all of the pictures in it."

Charlie asked, "What is a tomato box?"

She answered with exasperation, "It is a cardboard box with pictures of tomatoes on it. Damn boy, you really test me sometimes."

So, Charlie pulled down the stairs and went up into the attic.

She noticed that Tyler was drinking his tea, but hadn't tasted the fritters yet. She said, "Go on, taste one of those fritters."

Tyler did and was amazed.

She said "Ok, what did I put in mine that you didn't? Sandra snuck one of your fritters and I knew right away."

Tyler said "Cilantro, maybe... nutmeg. And scallions. I didn't use scallions."

She laughed heartily. "Lordy, Lordy. You are good, Tyler. I used just a pinch of cinnamon, not nutmeg."

Charlie came back into the room carrying the box of pictures. He placed them on a tray and put it in front of Aunt Pia. She started rummaging through the box, reached down into the bottom for a picture and finally came up with it.

She looked at the picture and murmured, "Mmm, Mmm, *Mmm*. If that doesn't beat all. I can't believe it is still here."

She showed the picture to Charlie and he said, "Oh, lord." He then handed it to Tyler and Tyler was floored. It was as though it was a picture of himself looking back, older, with white hair.

He stammered, "Who is this?"

"That is your g3 grandmother, Phoebe Thorne, sitting next to my great grandmother, Sarah Washington," Aunt Pia said. "This picture was high quality for the time and probably cost a good penny or two. Just look at those eyes and look at yours in the mirror. She was married to Virgil Thorne, and was an heiress to a shipping company in Philadelphia. You are a spitting image of her. Mmm, Mmm, Mmm. My word!"

Tyler was dumbfounded. He was one to never have been for a loss of words. This revelation stunned him. He didn't have any immediate family, and his extended family was spread out all over the country. They never had the close bond most families have. His Grandmother was about the only person he ever heard stories from; how he was named after her father and grandfather, but she moved away from Philadelphia when he was still young. When his parents were killed, there were only a couple of family members who attended the funeral. It was lonely for him, being the only child, and not having an extended family to lean on. The realization hit him now more so than when he lost his parents.

"Look at this!" She rummaged through and came up with a small bible inside of which was a family tree from that era.

"When I was 8 or 9 years old, my grandaddy started telling me stories about our family. I think he was pushing 85 himself. He started in chronological order, just like the bible, and went through the whole family. My mamma listened, my brothers and sisters listened, and we all remembered. Charlie's papa, God rest his soul, knew the most and did as much asking about town as he could. Even the family that moved back here from Philadelphia wanted to know everything.

"Aunt Pia," Charlie interrupted, chewing on a fritter, "we had family in Philadelphia?"

"Yes, we did. My great grandmother Sarah, Zack senior's wife, lived out her life with Phoebe Thorne in Philadelphia. They lived in the same house until they both passed. Sarah's oldest was also named Zack, and her grandson was Zack III, my father. Are you keeping up, Tyler?"

Tyler, still in shock, immediately said "Yes, indeed, Ma'am."

"Zack Jr. was my grandfather who told these stories. He was there. He must have been twelve or thirteen at the time. Virgil Thorne was killed towards the end of the war—that's the civil war; by a Yankee bummer, one of those rogues that robbed the country-side of food and family heirlooms. Sherman marched to the sea and then north into this area. Total surrender of the populace. Anyway, your g4 Virgil was killed by a bummer on the steps of his Daddy's plantation house just up the road from your house, Tyler. See, at the time, Virgil and Zack were like brothers. Zack Washington was a free man, as was all of our family. Virgil didn't keep slaves, but kept black workers, sort of indentured servitude. Zack and Virgil were thick as thieves and they had secrets, so everybody thought. Virgil and Phoebe built the house you now own. That house is your birthright, Tyler. When Virgil's daddy died before the war, for some reason, he and Phoebe and their kids moved into the big plantation house and Zack and his wife Sarah and kids moved into your house. Our family was in that house for over 120 years, until my other no good brother gambled it all away."

Charlie interrupted "Aunt Pia, forget him. Don't get riled up. He is not worth you getting upset again."

"I know Charlie," she said. "Tyler doesn't want to hear our dirty laundry. Help me up so I can use the restroom. Tyler, eat some more of those fritters before Charlie eats all of them. Boy, your mouth is always moving, one way or another."

Aunt Pia got up from her chair, grabbed her walker, and surprised Tyler by how quickly she was able to move with it. Charlie helped Aunt Pia to the bathroom, as much as she would let him, and came back into the living room.

"Tyler, I cannot believe what I'm hearing. We've heard stories, but never this much. Keep her talking. I'm going to call Sandra to come over and hear all of this."

Charlie picked up his cell phone, called Sarah, and hung up. He said "She is excited. She'll be here in about 3 minutes flat."

Just as Aunt Pia was coming back into the living room, Sandra came in.

Charlie was trying to help her into her chair and she shooed him off. As she was sitting down, she said, "Sandra, have I ever told you what a saint you are to have married this boy?"

Sandra answered, "Yes Pia, about three times a day."

Aunt Pia said "Try some of those fritters before Charlie eats all of them. Where was I?"

Tyler said, "You were talking about when Virgil was killed by the bummer and Zack and your family moved into the house."

Aunt Pia continued "Doesn't that beat all. You bought the house that your kin built. The Lord works in mysterious ways. Anyway, after Virgil was killed, Phoebe gathered her kids and moved to Philadelphia into her daddy's house."

Charlie showed Sandra the picture Tyler had been holding and she gasped.

"Tyler, you are a spitting image. My word!"

Aunt Pia said "Isn't that something. Those eyes have been passed down four generations and landed with Tyler. Anyway, as my grandaddy told it, one evening, Zack had sent Sarah and all of the kids over to his sister's house, except for Zack Jr. He may have been 14 years old or so. His daddy told him to stay in the house and out of sight. No matter what, he was not to come out of the house. He said it must have been about an hour later that some men rode up."

Aunt Pia hesitated a couple of seconds before saying, "I think I left out the most important part."

Sandra said "Take your time, Pia. We're listening."

Aunt Pia began again "Tyler, your house was once a stop on the underground railroad. You know what that was, right?"

"Yes Ma'am." he responded. "I think we all learned about it in school."

"Back then they called it the 'train', just like my grandaddy did," she continued. "He told us that Virgil and Zack hid over 250 people, sent them through the area to Elizabeth City, and from there, they took steamers north. Zack and Virgil even paid for their passage on the steamers. Those people had nothing and our kin clothed, fed them, and paid for their passage to freedom. All of them were in on it; Zack, Sarah, Virgil, and Phoebe. They used Phoebe's daddy's steamers to hide them on board during passage. It was all part of a big operation in this area. I told you, our families were very close back then."

Tyler, Charlie, and Sandra were all transfixed on Aunt Pia. She paused, took a sip of tea, and then continued.

"When those men rode up that night, all my great granddaddy heard was "Where is it, boy. Where you hiding it." Then he heard other muffled words and heard his daddy say 'I don't know. He died!' That was the last thing my granddaddy heard. Those men, the Klan, strung Zack up on that big oak tree at the back of the house. You know the one, Charlie!"

Tyler said "It's been cut down. There is only a massive stump."

Charlie said to Tyler "That tree must have been 350 years old. When it went down, the governor of the state had several desks made out of the cross cuts of the trunk. You are right. It was massive."

"After his funeral and burial," Aunt Pia continued, "Sarah moved two of her sisters into the house and she moved her kids to Philadelphia. They lived with Phoebe the rest of their lives. Sarah and Phoebe passed within a year of each other. Years later, Zack Jr. came back and claimed the house. Because of Phoebe's contacts in Philadelphia, no carpetbaggers ever got the property. Not so for the plantation house, which was burned, and 2000 acres. That property disappeared forever from the Thorne family. Phoebe and Sarah both made many trips back here. But really, it was too hard to stay, too many bad memories."

They were all too stunned to say anything. Hung from the tree? Klan? Carpetbaggers? Underground railroad? None of them had any idea how close they were to the history others only read in books. It all now became personal to Tyler.

Tyler asked sheepishly "Aunt Pia, may I have this picture?"

She nodded her head "Of course! It is your kin! I'll have Sandra get prints made."

Sandra looked right at Aunt Pia and said "I'm coming back here next week and you and I are going to go through all of these pictures, right down names and dates, and you are going to tell me any more stories you have. Why did you wait so long to tell this story?"

Aunt Pia pointed at Tyler and said, "His great grandfather was named Tyler Thorne Jr. I knew him. And I'm here to say you look a lot like him. He also had those eyes. These memories all came flooding back as soon as I looked into your eyes. Now Charlie, have you invited Tyler to Christmas dinner yet?"

Charlie said "No, Aunt Pia, not yet. If you would have given me the opportunity, I was going to invite him. You always try to take the thunder out of everything I do. You enjoy just making me look bad all the time. Something is wrong with you."

"Sandra, you are a saint," Aunt Pia said, and they all laughed while Charlie shook his head.

Chapter Nineteen

S ince there was a lull in the construction phase at the house, Tyler agreed to Josh and Ellie's plea to visit the culinary class at the High School. He had been in contact with the Principal, Mrs. Evans, and with the culinary teacher, Mr. Josephson. They both were thrilled to have him speak to the class. Both had attended the Children Fund event and were impressed by what he had done, especially with the students.

He scheduled the visit for Friday afternoon, so he'd be in town for the evening get-together at Millie's. He decided to wear nice jeans, loafers, a black t-shirt, and a blazer as a finishing touch. Through the scarred mirror in his bathroom, he figured he looked ok. A trimmed two day stubble to make himself look 'cosmopolitan' complemented his dark hair. His hair could have used a trim. It would be ok. Besides, he hadn't found the barber shop yet.

He thought in his mind, Serena is who he wanted to impress. He couldn't get her off of his mind. Why was that? A 6-year relationship had just ended, and here he was thinking of another woman. Then he thought he had never met anyone like her. She was pretty, accomplished, and had a heart of gold, just like Charlie had said. Tyler made mental notes all of the time and couldn't help comparing Serena to Jill, his ex-girlfriend. Jill was also accomplished, very good looking, street-wise, and had a natural way of making people feel welcome and comfortable. She was a people person, through and through.

On the other hand, given what had happened, he had found that Jill was also snobbish, distant towards him a lot of the time, self-centered, and extremely shallow—as with how their relationship ended. Serena had a bad temper and a potty mouth. She was not forthcoming in a crowd and liked to hang back, giving others the spotlight. Then he thought, he really liked that about her. Much of his career was out in front of people, and he always tried to let others take credit. It was always a joy for him to watch others bask in the spotlight, others that he knew he had helped get there.

Tyler arrived at the High School right after lunch, around 12:30. Mr. Josephson was in the test kitchen with about 40 students and teachers hanging around. Tyler couldn't believe the crowd. Mr. Josephson introduced Tyler to everyone and then said that the day's demonstration was on technique and presentation. He looked at Tyler and said "My class is made up of 18 students. Everyone else here came to watch and mainly to sample the end results."

Everyone laughed and Tyler started by introducing himself, quickly giving some of his background, and talked for at least 15 minutes about the job the students did at the gala. He described what orders they were given from him, how they carried them out, and what the end results had been. Josh yelled out "And then he made us clean up." Everyone laughed, which was a real ice breaker.

With the food selected and the ingredients reviewed, they began. At 4:30, Mr. Josephson interrupted and said it was getting late. They weren't quite done, but he said they had to wrap it up. No one wanted to leave. Teachers were coming and going in the kitchen. At 5:30, all presentations were done and everyone sampled and ate and reviewed what the students had created.

Mr. Josephson cornered Tyler.

"What you just did was just short of amazing. These are teenagers and you held their attention for 5 hours, as well as teachers in and out, chattering about it. This, firsthand, is what creates the romanticism surrounding the restaurant business. I can't thank you enough for the boost of morale. They'll be talking about it for months. You have to come back again."

"Believe it or not," Tyler said, "I had a blast today. These kids are very impressionable and how they are introduced into the business is the key to their future success. You need to be commended on how you handled the ingredients, direction, and Josh, on a couple of occasions. I tip my hat to you."

Mr. Josephson said "Coming from you, Tyler, it is a real compliment. Thank you! And regarding Josh, I know his parents very well. Small town. He's been like that forever. You just have to know how to push his buttons."

Tyler looked at his watch and said, "I hate to leave but it's 6PM. Would you mind if I said my goodbyes?"

"Not at all."

Chapter Twenty

T yler arrived at Millie's about 20 minutes after 6PM and saw a group of about twelve standing around the bar. He approached them and Barbara and Janice both broke off to greet him.

"My oh my, if it isn't Mr. Tyler himself." Barbara said. Janice joined in "And isn't he looking spiffy in his sports coat," touching the lapels and pockets.

"Stop it, you two." Tyler said. "I was at the High School today fulfilling a promise I made to the students to visit them there. Ends up they had me cooking all afternoon."

The ladies took him over to their group and introduced everyone. They ordered him a glass of wine and a couple of them shot questions at him about the fundraiser, the food, and everything that took place. He was talking to them all when Serena walked in. She was wearing her work clothes still, which were a little muddy. As she approached the group, she saw Tyler's profile and went white. Barbara and Janice edged over to her.

Barbara started in on her by saying "Your friend is here." Janice chimed in "And he is looking *good*!"

Serena looked at Barbara and said in a tight lipped, "You did this, didn't you?"

"Well, yes, I did. I invited him and thought you would be happy about it, you ingrate."

Tight-lipped again, Serena said "Look at me. I'm filthy, have mud in my hair, and have been sweating all day. A little heads-up would have been *nice.*"

"You look fine." Barbara responded. "Not like you did in that dress the other night. But I don't think he'll really care."

Billy came over to the three and said, "Nice look, Serena." She shot him a snarl. He continued "Are you a good witch, or a bad witch tonight," at which she countered "I'm a sandwich, Billy. Bite me."

Janice interrupted "Billy, please get Serena a glass of wine." He said 'ok' and snarled back at her.

Serena said, "Seriously, I can't stay here like this."

Tyler came up to them with a glass of wine and handed it to Serena.

"Billy told me to deliver this to you. He is such a nice guy, Janice. You are lucky to have him."

"Isn't she though," Serena interjected, dripping with not-too-subtle sarcasm.

Tyler looked at Serena and said, "Rough day?"

Barbara and Janice ambled off quietly.

"Yes, and I came here for a quick drink. I look like shit," Serena answered.

Tyler said immediately "You look fine. I just came from the High School and had to clean up for the students. I haven't worn a jacket in months."

"You look good, Tyler," she said. And they joined the others.

After about thirty minutes of banter, laughs, and stories, Tyler and Serena sat at a booth and started to talk. Tyler knew not to get personal with her, but to keep the conversation light and flowing. No weird pauses. No weird vibes. Just two friends talking.

He didn't have to worry. Serena was delightful, full of questions, and questions he was glad to answer. Nothing serious.

"Tyler, not to get too personal, but why Edenton?" was one of her questions. "I mean, Barbara made us all read the article about you and I get it. But you could have relocated anywhere. Why here?"

Tyler started "Honest question. When I was in college my major was history. My father and grandfather were both lawyers. It was preordained for me to follow into their profession. But I really liked history. And I hated law. It just wasn't in my makeup. One summer, a buddy of mine that lived in this area was going to spend the break here metal detecting all of the beaches and some of the swampy areas. I have always loved metal detecting. It's been a hobby since I was a kid. My dad and I spent hours traipsing through the woods in Pennsylvania, looking for whatever we could find. Anyway, my grandmother had told me that some of our ancestors had come from this area and she knew the area and its history. She encouraged me not only to do my metal detecting, but to look up some of my family history."

Serena asked, "You had family here?"

Tyler replied," Oh yes. And that is a whole different story. Anyway, I spent a whole summer here metal detecting, drinking beer, and chasing college coeds. It probably was the best summer of my life. We stayed at his parents' house. But, most of the time, we metal detected, camped, canoed, and swam. When we got bored, we went down to Wilmington around the college there and chased women."

Serena chuckled, "I remember those days in between semesters. They make memories that are hard to forget. So, what's the draw to metal detecting around here? Pirate booty?"

Tyler looked shocked and said, "You know about pirate treasure?"

Serena laughed and said "We all grew up hearing the stories of buried treasure. But we thought they were a load of bunk."

Tyler, very seriously, answered, "Well, they aren't. The pirate stories are real, but the buried treasure is lore."

Some of the others joined them at the booth and carried on, like most people do on a Friday night with drinks flowing. They welcomed Tyler as part of the group and he sincerely appreciated their friendship, banter, and fellowship. Not that he didn't take his turn. Billy quickly dubbed him 'Mr. Chef' and they all teased him about the tall hats, the white smocks, why he wasn't on 'Master-Chef or Hell's Kitchen' on TV, and so on. He quipped back and forth with them and they enjoyed it. His adage was always 'if you can't take the heat, get out of the kitchen.' He also threw a couple of zingers out there himself. He asked why the town had internet service when they already had inter-Barbara service. Barbara responded by cussing Charlie.

He hadn't laughed as much in months. At about 11PM Serena came up to him and said, "Hey, I have to go. Tomorrow, I have an 8AM meeting at the courthouse and then I'm heading to my brother's house in Charlotte for Christmas. I gave the crew a paid week off and am going to spend 3 or 4 days there. What are you doing for Christmas? You cannot be alone! Tyler, tell me you have plans?"

Tyler said "Charlie and Sandra invited me to spend Christmas day with them. Well, really, Aunt Pia invited me and Charlie got mad because she stole his thunder."

Serena laughed and said, "You met Aunt Pia?"

Tyler said "Yes, that's the second part of the story I mentioned about family in this area. She is like a living encyclopedia. Unbelievable at her age, how sharp she is and her memory."

"Well, now you have my interest stoked. I want to hear all about it when I get back. They don't make them like Aunt Pia anymore. I have spent hours with her just listening and prodding her for information."

Tyler said, "I guess if you watch her stories with her she will tell you anything."

Serena's eyes got wide "You really do know her, don't you? You will have the best day of your life with that family. They are like my second family. One bit of advice: Don't cook anything. They will have twenty family members there and about another ten guests. Sandra loves to cook and put out a spread; thirty people there and enough food to feed a hundred. I'm telling you. I've been there.

Take a couple bottles of wine and a good liquor, single malt scotch if you can. At least you will be tops in Charlie's book."

"I can't thank you enough for that advice." Tyler said. "I know just what to buy for Charlie. He is always going on about single malt scotch. Anything else?"

"Last thing," Serena added. "You really got me interested in that pirate stuff and your family history. I'm serious. When I get back, we need to talk about it. Aunt Pia is amazing. Her stories are revelations more than stories."

Tyler smiled "I'd love to. I'll call you when you get back."

CHAPTER TWENTY-ONE

C harlie's house was a large, two-story Victorian that was very well done. It was white and had hunter green shutters and a subtle green trim throughout, and it was evident that Charlie had spent a lot of time and money on the house and grounds. There was a detached two-car garage and workshop combination, plenty of room for woodworking and projects.

Tyler went in and was warmly welcomed by everyone, introduced to the kids and grandkids, and some of the other guests; most of whom he met at the fundraiser.

He walked into the kitchen and gave Sandra a kiss on the cheek and heard Aunt Pia say, "I hope I get one of those kisses." She was sitting at the end of the kitchen table, holding court, with all of her great, great nephews and nieces hovering about her.

"Of course." Tyler said. "I'm saving the biggest one for you."

"You are a devil, aren't you?" Aunt Pia joked.

"I try," he responded.

He went over and kissed her on the cheek. Charlie said, "What do you have there, Tyler?"

Tyler walked over to Sandra and said, "I have two bottles of red, two bottles of white, and two special bottles for Charlie."

Sandra said "Uh, oh."

Charlie chuckled, opening up the bag, and said 'Lordy!"

Aunt Pia said "Boy, if that's single malt, you better not hide it. Crack that puppy open right now."

"Aunt Pia," Charlie started, "You are only getting one drink and that is it. You cannot drink this with the medication you are on."

She responded, a little loudly, "I know how much I can drink. I'm 95 years old and if you don't open that bottle, I'll open it upside your head."

One of the small kids yelled into the living room, "Daddy, PapPap is in trouble with Aunt Pia again."

They all laughed and Charlie just shook his head.

"You know, Tyler," Sandra commented, "When the kids were little, Charlie used to wonder what was for dinner and I wondered what we were going to drink at dinner. Now it has reversed. I worry about dinner and Charlie can't wait for that glass of wine."

Aunt Pia said, "He needs to drink more wine, to mellow him out."

The entire dinner and day was the same: laughs, love, and general good nature. Charlie showed Tyler his workshop and some of the projects he had done there. Tyler was truly impressed. That type of workmanship is hard to find today. Charlie was good at what he did.

Back in the kitchen, sipping on some wine, Sandra asked "So, you were out with the gang two nights ago?"

Tyler said "Yes, and I had a wonderful time. Didn't leave until close to midnight."

Sandra kept on "Was Serena there?"

Tyler questioningly said, "*Yes.*"

"Did you talk to her?"

"*Yes.*"

"And did you ask her out?"

"Sandra, stop it." Charlie interrupted. "I forbade Tyler from messing with her. He knows he has to answer to me if he messes with her."

Sandra got angry. "Charlie, she is a woman and she has feelings, just like everyone else. She has had a rough time with relationships, ok. Is she to be alone forever? And, Tyler has had a rough time too. I'm sorry, Tyler. I read the article. No offense."

"None taken," Tyler said.

"If these two young people want to interact, who in the hell are you to stop it?"

Charlie raised his hands in surrender. "I give up. Between you and Pia, I'm just going to drink my scotch."

Aunt Pia said under her breath "About time you got some smarts."

"We are supposed to get together at Millie's and finish a conversation we started on Friday," Tyler said.

"You call her tonight, wish her a Merry Christmas, and ask her out on New Year's Eve." Sandra said. "Her gang always goes out in couples and for once she'll be able to join them. It's a little underhanded way of getting her out on New Year's Eve with her friends."

Aunt Pia said, "Sandra, I think Charlie learned all his mischief from you. That is pretty good logic, Tyler, if you ask me."

Charlie said, "No one asked you."

"I'll call her tonight." Tyler answered. "And by the way, Aunt Pia, I really like her. She is a good person."

Aunt Pia said "I know she is. And you got a thing for her!"

Tyler grinned a big grin.

That evening, at home, he called Serena and wished her a Merry Christmas.

"My nieces and nephews wore me out today. It was great. I really needed some family time." She talked for about fifteen minutes. "Now, tell me all about Sandra and Charlie's. Was it fun?"

They talked for over an hour. Finally, Tyler 'formally' asked her out for New Year's and she accepted.

"Let me get with inter-Barbara, find out what is going on, and I'll let you know." They laughed and hung up.

Serena laid on her bed and thought, *Do I do this? I really like him. But I haven't had sex in two years? Oh, well, third time's a charm.*

Tyler laid on his bed and thought, *Do I do this? It's only been eight months since the whole breakup.* But then he thought no, it was longer than that. The intimacy had been gone much longer than eight months and lord knows, he was ready for some intimacy.

Sandra and Charlie laid in bed that night reviewing the great day they just had. Charlie was tired, had too much scotch, and was trying to go to sleep.

"Charlie, I know you protect her like she was one of your own."

"She is one of my own," Charlie responded.

"I know," Sandra replied, "but she is a grown woman and she needs someone. Tyler is perfect for her, even Pia sees that."

Charlie mumbled, "Pia can't see shit."

"You know what I mean. Don't discourage her if they hook up. Promise me."

CHAPTER TWENTY-TWO

The week after Christmas, Tyler found an energy he hadn't had in a long time. Within two days, the electricians had finished wiring the entire house. The plumbers had finished the septic system and most of the new pipes and drains had been installed. They worked so quickly it spun his head. All of them wanted the long weekend for New Year's. And Tyler paid them all extra just to get the job done. By Wednesday night, the house was starting to take on a new life, and Tyler finally had hot water that was hot enough to take a decent bath. It was worth every penny he paid extra just to take a hot bath. Installing a shower was part of phase two of the project once he started remodeling the entire upstairs. The HVAC wasn't anywhere near complete, and with the current cold front, he piled extra blankets on his bed.

The entire week, all he thought about was Serena. She wasn't getting back until Thursday. They talked each evening under the pretense of 'How's the project going?' But they both knew that talking to each other was anticipated every night.

Friday night they all met at Millie's at 6PM and had drinks. The main topic of conversation was Saturday night, New Year's Eve. Of course, Barbara took control of the event.

"Ok," she started, "we all meet here at 7PM for drinks and to see who looks the best."

They all laughed; but she was right. It was a tradition to not be formal, but wear really nice clothes, like kids playing dress-up. New Year's Eve you had to sparkle to bring in the new year.

She continued "At 9PM, we go over to Janice's parents' house for the traditional hot toddy. At 11PM, we all go to Tyler's house for the grand tour, isn't that right, Tyler."

He nodded.

"We bring in the new year there and party till dawn."

Janice injected "Party till dawn? Are you crazy? I haven't been up past midnight since last New Year's Eve."

Barbara said "The kids are staying at my mother's, and Craig and I have a free night out. We are going to make the most of it."

Tyler said "Sounds like a great plan to me. I'll even provide breakfast."

So, it was settled. That was the plan. There would be six couples in all.

Everyone chatted about the big night for a while, until it died down and Tyler and Serena found themselves alone.

Serena teased, "Ok, Captain Ahab, Aaargh. You never finished your metal-detecting pirate story last time we were here," trying to sound like a pirate.

"Don't laugh." Tyler answered. "I took it very seriously then; and I still do. There really could be pirate treasure hidden around here."

"You would really waste time with that detector looking for a needle in a pile of needles?" she countered. "Sounds far-fetched."

Tyler said "I didn't say I was going to make it my career. I said it was a hobby, nothing more."

"Why do you think there still could be treasure out there somewhere?" Serena asked.

Tyler began, "I have a degree in history and it's the history behind piracy. In the late 17th century and early 18th century, sometimes called the Golden Age of Piracy, pirates frequented the east coast of the colonies—From around 1680 up to around 1725 was the timeframe.[1] The colonists welcomed the pirates with open arms. The pirates would loot and rob mainly the Spanish in the Caribbean. First it was gold and silver. If there were no precious metals on board a captured ship, they'd rob whatever cargo the ship had. Sugar, molasses, flour, and rum were always favorites. They would come back to the colonies and sell their booty to be able to resupply their ships. The colonies were tied to England for all trade. Taxes and tariffs made the 'free' pirate merchandise very attractive, and stimulated the economy throughout the entire east coast. They even took personal items of clothing and hats, purses, and coats from passengers, since most passengers were of the wealthier classes and had nice clothing. They sold the clothing to colonists for big money. Once the pirates got paid by their captains, they'd drink and holler for a couple of days in whatever town they were in, spending a big portion of their shares. Sometimes they ransomed prisoners. Very seldom did they kill whomever they captured; those killed were usually the result of a fight. All of this activity stimulated the local economies."[2]

"Like I said, the colonists accepted them with open arms. After the Spanish started protecting their ships with warships in the Caribbean, the pirates made their way to the Indian Ocean and started raiding Mughal ships, which carried silk, spices, and gems, more so than gold and silver. And some of the pirates would always return to the east coast of America with whatever merchandise they had."[3]

In 1695, the greatest heist ever recorded took place at the confluence of the Red Sea and the Gulf of Aden, near present-day Yemen and Djibouti. A pirate named Henry Every, or sometimes called Avery, had a 40-gun ship, called The Fancy, and with one other ship, captured two Mughal ships returning from the yearly pilgrimage to Mecca.[4] In the early 17th century, the Netherlands and Germany developed the art of faceting gemstones, which is currently used today.[5] The Mughals had gems from India and China, but they were not faceted. Almost 100 years later, the Mughals certainly would have heard of this art and seen the resulting work.

I do not know if this is a fact—whether there was an arranged meeting with artisans from Europe in the Middle East or not; but the largest ship of that group of pilgrims was also a treasure ship. It was well armed and had a contingent of soldiers with rifles to protect the ship. Avery attacked with his ship and his first volley brought the main mast down. Then one of the Mughal cannons on deck exploded and fire swept through the ship. It was boarded and captured, with an estimated £300,000 to £600,000 of treasure on board. This was not just bullion or coin. It was precious gems and jewelry fashioned by these early artisans.[6] This time, the pirates went crazy with the captured ship. They raped and tortured the pilgrims, some of whom were related to the Mughal emperor himself.

While Avery was discussing splitting the loot with the other Captain, an argument ensued and Avery snuck away during the night with the entire treasure.

The Mughal Emperor was enraged and had executives of the East India company arrested. And the East India Company was to blame for not protecting Mughal ships. The East India Company retaliated and also got the English Government involved. Both outfitted and sent warships to the Indian Ocean and to the east coast of the colonies.

Avery was in the Bahamas when news arrived that he was the most wanted man in the world. Then he disappeared. Rumors circulated for years after his disappearance, but neither he nor his treasure were ever found.[7] He not only had performed one of the biggest heists in history, he also was one of the few pirates who got away with his treasure. Most ended up at the end of a rope, or were killed in brutal circumstances. This incident, along with pirating in general and British Warships, is what eventually brought down the pirates, around 1725 or so."[8]

Tyler took a drink of his wine and continued. "There are a couple of local characters that are worth noting, and on whom I've done a ton of research. The first one is William Teach, otherwise known as..."

Serena interrupted "Blackbeard."

Tyler said "Yes, Blackbeard. You get another glass of wine for that correct answer," and he waved to Todd for 2 more glasses.

Tyler quizzically said "You want me to continue? It feels like I'm giving a lecture on our first date."

Serena said "In college, I had several history classes and the best subjects were those that involved this region of the country. I knew about Charles Eden and the pirates. And, I also know some of the history of sweet potatoes, believe it or not. I find this all very interesting."

Tyler thought, *Wow! She is actually into this. She's great!*

Todd delivered their wine and Tyler continued. "The other pirate was Stede Bonnet. He and Teach pirated together and it was sort of an uneasy alliance. Neither trusted the other; but together, they were making a ton of loot. Both were friends with the governor at the time, Charles Eden. The capital of North Carolina was Bath, just north of here. Then the capital switched to here, Edenton, in 1722. Then to New Bern in 1743, and finally to Raleigh in 1792. Charles Eden pardoned both Teach and Bonnet in 1718 and Teach settled in Bath, where he bought a house. He eventually took up pirating again and was captured and hung for it. The point is that he and Bonnet both spent a lot of time here and Teach scuttled his ship, Queen Anne's Revenge, in Ocracoke inlet. His fortune was never found." [9]

Serena interjected "So, you and 1000 others think they hid treasure here."

Tyler said, "Here, or in the surrounding area."

"Well, I stand by my initial assessment. It is like trying to find a needle in a stack of needles."

"Of course, it is," Tyler had to admit. "But it is a hobby and I had a blast that summer doing it. When the house is finished, I'll probably take it up again."

Serena said "To be honest, it sounds like a worthwhile hobby.

Visiting different parts of this area would be fun. And, you'd have a reason to visit. Would you take me along sometime?"

"Of course. I'd love to." Tyler said genuinely. "The fun is in the hunt, not really finding anything."

Serena thought, '*What a refreshing attitude. This guy is really different.*

CHAPTER TWENTY-THREE

Saturday night was a great time. The ladies were all dressed and looked fabulous. It was cold out, unseasonably cold for that area of the country. The temperature dipped into the teens. All of the females had communicated and agreed to wear pants suits with sparkly accessories. Tyler had picked up Serena at her apartment and she came to the door wearing khaki dress slacks with a total outfit that was stunning. She turned and grabbed her coat. *Wow,* he thought. *What a body.* She was the whole package: sassy, smart, independent, and gorgeous. They headed to Millie's. They all gathered, had a drink, and then went to Janice's parents' house.

Her parents' house was similar to Caroline Jackson's house. It was large and had a roomy formal area that made it perfect for get-togethers. There was a mix of a crowd that made for a very pleasant evening. Her parents doted over Tyler since he was the star of the fundraiser.

Billy grabbed Tyler later and said, "I'm going to marry their daughter and they looked at you as though *you* were going to. I may have to take cooking classes."

Tyler said, "Billy, if you want to make an impression, impress her mom. Buy her some flowers or do something really sappy and she'll come around much faster than her dad. You bring the mom around the dad will have to follow. He has no choice. In the restaurants I've been associated with, the female always makes the choices as to where to sit, whom to invite, what to order, and always sets the agenda. Look at Charlie. He doesn't stand a chance with the women in his life, and neither do we in the long run."

"Don't I know it." Billy concurred. "One more thing, Tyler. You are really good for Serena. She has been smiling all night. And, she hasn't cussed me out since before Christmas."

Tyler broke out laughing. "Come to think of it, her potty mouth has subsided, hasn't it?"

"Yes, it has," he quickly finished because Serena walked up to them. Billy said, as he took his leave, "I guess you do have pants other than jeans!"

Serena started to respond; but she stopped, looked at Tyler, and said, "No, not tonight."

Tyler joked, "Are you feeling ok? I never thought I'd see you pass up a chance throwing a barb back at Billy."

"You have no idea how good I feel. I am out on New Year's Eve with my friends, at a party, and dressed up in clothes other than jeans and a t-shirt," she said. "And, I happen to be with a very handsome man," grabbing his arm.

"Flattery will get you everywhere," Tyler said with a smile. Her touch sent shivers up his back. Wow, he thought, he was *totally hooked*. He kept thinking— *Go slow. Don't scare her away.*

At around 11PM, Janice's group broke off to leave the older folks alone. They all headed to Tyler's house to bring in the New Year. He had worked all day setting things up.

He warned them all about the mud at the right side of the driveway. The septic field went off the right side of the house down the gradual slope. They all entered the foyer and stood there looking around. He went into the big room where he had a small bar set up, some tables, and some nice chairs. He asked Craig to open the wine while he retrieved some ice. What he had noticed with this group, and what he liked, was the fact that none of them drank to excess.

They liked having drinks, but getting drunk was not part of it. That was so refreshing.

When he came back and everyone had a drink, he started the tour. Upstairs first, to show the bedrooms. The guest room was fully furnished and his bedroom was fully furnished. The other bedrooms were empty, except for a couple of boxes. In one was his metal detector, which took about fifteen minutes of explaining. It involved his college story again.

The bathroom was a topic of conversation because of the ancient clawfoot bathtub. He told them a shower was coming soon. When they went into the attic, Serena made a comment that she was really impressed with the work Charlie had done on the beams and roof. She said only someone of Charlie's caliber could have done what he did so well and so quickly. Billy agreed and made his own comments on the workmanship.

He showed them the rest of the downstairs and finally, they made their way into the kitchen. Barbara asked to use the restroom and Tyler pointed to the closet. She opened the door and said "No way am I going in there with all of you standing right here."

Tyler said laughing "Please use the one upstairs. This closet has been the butt of all jokes since I moved in: no pun intended."

Group groan!

He showed them the kitchen and talked about the plans for it. Craig said "Tyler, not to be too personal—This is a large house and I know the amount of money you are going to sink into it. Have you really thought about it, I mean financially? You'll probably never get your money back out of it. You don't have to answer if it's too personal."

"No Craig, it's a good question," Tyler answered with no qualms about it. "And I have really thought hard about it. Bottom line, I might dump everything I made off the restaurant into it. Maybe not. Whatever happens, this is going to be my home. I'm here to stay. In the end, I want the house to be mine and whatever changes happen, I will know I made them. If I have to work two jobs for the rest of my life, then so be it."

Barbara and Janice both did a side glance to Serena, which she saw. Both grinned. Later, Barbara told Serena "I told you, he is a keeper. You better jump his bones before someone else does."

Serena said, "In good time. I still have to feel him out a little bit. I'm not sure how damaged he is yet. If I make a move and it's too quick, it could really hurt our relationship in the long run."

Midnight came with the countdown and everyone was enjoying themselves. After the countdown, Tyler had several hot plates hooked up in the kitchen and made home fries, toast, and individual omelets for everyone, which took only minutes with the hotplates going full throttle. Serena somewhat helped him and was amazed at his skill and dexterity. They all ate and chatted incessantly. Around 1AM everyone started to fizzle. Barbara and Craig said their goodbyes. Janice said with a wink that Billy had too much to drink, and she had to get him home. Everyone else said their goodbyes. Before she left, Barbara purposely said to Serena, while Tyler was next to her, "Do you want us to drop you off???"

Serena said "No, Thanks. I want to help Tyler clean up and I think he'll take me home, won't you?"

Tyler said "Of course."

Barbara grinned a wide grin and said, "Don't do anything I would do." And they left.

Serena helped with the dishes and the utensils and, in fifteen minutes, they were done. Tyler held up a bottle of wine and said, "How about a Cabernet nightcap?"

Serena said 'sure' and they sat on the couch with their wine.

CHAPTER TWENTY-FOUR

Serena started by saying, "the week before Christmas you had mentioned you had family here at one time, something Aunt Pia told you?"

Tyler told her the entire story. As she listened, she asked some questions and tried to piece the puzzle together. When Tyler was done, it was late.

Serena said, "Tyler, I am very, very interested in this story. But I think I need to hear it again. It is very complicated and Aunt Pia tends to leave things out. I've had too much wine and it is, Oh my God, 2:00AM! I need to get home."

"Not tonight." Tyler offered, "My guest room is fully functional. I have extra pajamas, and I bought one of those toothbrush packs that have about 200 toothbrushes in them; you'll find them in the bathroom. Serves me right for buying from the wholesale club. Anyway, neither one of us should drive. Please, no strings. Just a bed."

She accepted the offer. They went upstairs and Tyler showed her the room again, where everything was, and added, "Leave your door open. I do it every night. The heat is not up to par yet and the open door will allow the heat to get into the room. I put an extra blanket on the bed."

Serena got undressed, put on the pajamas Tyler gave her, rolled up the sleeves and legs, and whisked to the bathroom in her socks. She brushed her teeth, did her business, and whisked back to her room, across the hall and a few stair steps from Tyler's. She laid in bed and dozed off.

Tyler heard her whisk through the hallway and welcomed the noise in the house. Each night was quiet except for the creaking of the old house. Having another person in the house made it feel just a little more comfortable.

At 3AM, Tyler felt some movement in his bed. He partially rolled over and saw Serena was crawling under his covers. She saw him looking and said "This house is fucking freezing. Don't even think about it. Roll over and go back to sleep," which he did.

At 8AM, he was awakened by Serena shuffling off to the bathroom. She came back into bed with her back to him, in the middle of the king-sized bed. Tyler was awake now and he turned and moved closer to Serena. He spooned her and wrapped his arm over and around her body, ending with his hand cupped under her breast.

Serena said, "That's not my hand you're holding."

Tyler said "Since you basically slept on top of me all of last night, I figured I was due this cuddle. And besides, that's not my leg up against your butt."

She giggled and said, "You are full of shit."

To which he replied, "Speaking of full of shit, *Ms.* Lesbian."

Serena said "Barbara started that rumor to keep the wolves at bay. How did you know?"

Tyler countered "The night of the fundraiser. I saw you in that dress and I *just*, somehow knew."

Serena said "Billy calls that my 'fuck me' dress. Every time I wear it, guys want to fuck me."

"Well, he's right and I did. And Charlie told me anyway," Tyler said.

Serena turned over and their faces were about six inches apart. She looked at Tyler and said "There is something I have wanted to do ever since the first day we met at my truck. Morning wine breath and all." She kissed him long and deep. They broke off and Tyler said "*Wow*" very softly. After a second, he said, "There is a hint of currants and maybe some blackberries."

Serena giggled.

Tyler continued, "And there is something I have wanted to do since we met at your truck." He kissed her and, in one motion, boosted her up onto his chest and wrapped each hand on each of her butt cheeks. "You have the most amazing butt I have ever seen. I've wanted to do that forever."

She responded, "That's not the only amazing thing I have." Then she added, "Tyler, it has been a long time for me, over two years."

"It has been a long time for me too," Tyler said. "Not just in time, but also in intimacy."

They made love, the slow and purposeful kind of love that only comes with a sincere desire. After about forty-five minutes, they came up for air.

Tyler said, "That was everything I thought it would be, I dreamed it would be. You are an amazing woman, Serena Milner."

She replied, "And you are an amazing man, Tyler Harrington."

They lay in bed in an embrace for a while.

"How about some coffee and toast?" Tyler offered.

"Sounds like a plan."

They got dressed and, while she was putting on her pajamas, she said "What's with these pajamas, anyway? You only had a t-shirt and shorts on in this freezing house."

"I've had those for years." Tyler explained. "My ex got them for me one Christmas but I never wore them."

Serena blurted "Jesus Christ, Tyler. You gave me pajamas your ex bought? Give me a shirt and some sweats. I'm not wearing these."

They both laughed and he gave her a shirt and sweats, which she floated in, but looked extremely sexy.

They made coffee and toast and chatted about a host of topics. After the coffee was gone and the toast finished, he looked up and saw her bending over the sink putting the dirty napkins in the trash. He got up, stripped her naked, and they went at it again in the kitchen, this time a little more urgently.

Then they decided to take a bath, made love again, and stayed there until the water went cold and the skin in their fingers started to shrivel.

Mostly spent, they laid on the couch and talked. He reviewed what they had talked about the night before, discussing it at length most of the afternoon. Serena was able to make better sense of all of the g2's and g3's. They decided to order Chinese and stay in for the evening. During that time, Sandra called and Serena talked to her a little bit. Tyler went up to the bathroom and Sandra asked what she was doing.

"I'm at Tyler's house," Serena said.

"You aren't working today, are you?"

"*No,*" Serena answered

"Girl, you tell me right now. Did you spend the night?" Sandra asked quite directly.

"*Yes,*" came the sheepish reply.

"And you..."

"*Yes.*"

"Oh, my word, I am so happy for you," Sandra said.

Serena giggled. "Tell Aunt Pia her afternoon nap dream came true, and I think mine did too."

Tyler came in and nodded to the phone and mouthed,

"Who is that?"

"Sandra," Serena mouthed back.

"She knows?"

And Serena nodded. As Serena said her goodbyes on the phone, Tyler said "Charlie will kick my ass tomorrow."

"No, he won't," she reassured him. "Sandra will keep him in line."

They were eating the Chinese feast he ordered when Serena's phone rang.

"Oh no. It's Barbara, for the fifth time."

"Well, there's no time like the present," Tyler said.

"Hello."

She heard "You slut. I called Sandra to see if you were there, since you wouldn't answer your phone, and turn my head for two seconds, and you are bed-hopping. I want all of the dirty details and I want them now."

Serena had opened the phone so Tyler could listen.

She simply responded, "Bye, Barbara. I'll call you in the morning. We're finishing our Chinese food right now."

As she was hanging up, she heard, "No, you call me tonight."

"Well," Serena said, "we are officially an item and the town gossip for the next two weeks or so, or until we are seen out in public together.

"Well," Tyler challenged, "we could really be the gossip if they found out about my new record of four times in one day. Let's see, bedroom, kitchen, bathroom . . . all we have left is the living room. And here we are!"

They went at it again. Afterwards, they got dressed and Tyler drove Serena into town to her apartment. Tyler said, "Mind if I see your place?" She answered immediately, "No way are we going for five. I'm spent."

"That's not what I had in mind," Tyler said, "But I do like the way you think."

CHAPTER TWENTY-FIVE

The next morning Charlie arrived early and Tyler was waiting for him. Tyler stepped onto the front porch with two coffee mugs.

Charlie said, "Oh, so the rabbit came out of his hutch?"

"Don't start on me Charlie. Seriously, I think I'm in love," Tyler responded.

Charlie said "No, that's the sex talking. Give it time. You don't know love until you're up against it or if you have to deal with the women in your life. Go slow."

"Is that you talking, or Sandra talking," Tyler asked.

"Shit, that's me talking. Sandra and Pia already have you and Serena filling this house with kids."

"Charlie, it was freezing in here last night, the temperature I mean." Tyler said grinning, as Charlie shook his head. "Let's talk today about the duct work and what has to happen."

"We'll have to remove all of those radiators before we can get rid of that old boiler," Charlie went into work mode. "Then we have to run the ductwork throughout the basement and then into the ceilings for the upstairs unit. How are you going to live with no heat?"

"Don't worry about me. It's supposed to warm up next week and I'm going to buy a large space heater for my bedroom. While you do that, I'm going to work on that kitchen monster of a fireplace."

"It's amazing, after all of this time, those fireplaces are in better shape than some built five years ago. They did it right back then," Charlie reflected.

They did their own thing all morning. After lunch, Charlie said he'd knock off around 3PM for a dentist appointment. Tyler was still working on the fireplace and told Charlie he'd be working on it the rest of the day.

In the late afternoon, Tyler had cleaned and scraped most of the dirt and grime around the outside of the fireplace. He loved it. It was almost five feet deep and eight feet wide. It was huge. The hearth was about 30 inches deep, as was the firebox itself. There were two iron hangers on each side of the outside of the firebox that swiveled to the front, over the hearth. These were used for hanging pots to cook meals. The outer left and outer right side of the fireplace were covered by large oak panels, split halfway up, that rose to eye level, capped by an oak mantle. The panels and the mantle were never painted and, although faded, he knew they could be sanded and brought back to life. The entire structure was impressive work.

Charlie had told him that all of the flues had to be cleaned again, and the entire kitchen flue relined, if they wanted to use the fireplace. There was an additional firebox in the bedroom above, which used the same flue.

Looking up into the flue, he noticed another flue coming from below. He figured it was an air vent. He also saw a nail sticking out of the inside of the chimney, with no apparent use. It was large, more a spike than a nail, and had a round head instead of a flat head. He tried to work it free but it was stuck. He banged it softly with a hammer, so as not to ruin the mortar in between the bricks. If there was a hole left, he could fix it later. It finally loosened and when it did move, it came towards him about six inches. His first reaction was that he had ruined the mortar, but then he heard a loud 'clunk' on the left side of the fireplace. He thought that the nail might have gone through the wood. He got out of the firebox and went around to the left side of the structure. There was dust settling and he saw the bottom panel had come loose on three sides. He froze. The top and bottom of the lower panel had wood pieces that looked like handles. They matched the top panel so the two together were symmetrical. But looking at them closer now, they really looked like handles. He pushed and the entire panel swung inward, showing a two-ft gap in the fireplace with a ladder leading down into black space.

Tyler gathered his wits and decided what to do. He wasn't going into that hole alone. He knew Charlie was busy. He called Serena.

"Serena, I need you to come over," Tyler said.

Serena said "Tyler, I'm tired. There is no way we can go at it again tonight."

Tyler chuckled "That's not why I need you to come over, although I do like the way you think. I found something. You have to come over."

"What did you find?"

I can't explain it. Just come over."

It took Serena about thirty minutes to get there. While he was waiting, Tyler grabbed the handle and swung the door back into place. He heard the nail click again. He reached up into the fireplace and once again, with some effort, the nail moved and the panel opened. He closed the door once again.

When Serena got there, they gave each other a hug and an extended, sensual kiss. Tyler broke off and excitedly said,

"Later for that. You have to see this."

He showed the light up into the fireplace and said "Look at the flue. Go up about two feet and what do you see?"

She said "A hole? Maybe an air vent?"

Tyler said, "That's what I thought. Now look to the left at that large spike sticking out of the wall." She did and he continued "Now, go stand on the left side of the fireplace."

She said "Come on, Tyler. What is this?"

"Please, humor me," he begged.

She went around the side of the fireplace and Tyler pulled the spike. The clunk opened the panel and Tyler went around and saw Serena standing there with her mouth open. He pushed the door all of the way open and they both looked into the cobweb filled hole.

The hole was about two feet wide and was lined with bricks from the fireplace, all of the way down into the darkness below.

Serena said "I'll be right back. Get a broom." She ran out to her truck and came back with two halogen work lamps and an extension cord. They plugged the lamps in and peered into the hole.

Serena said, "go down there and clean the cobwebs as you descend."

Tyler said "I'm not going down there first. You go first."

"You big ass baby. I pay people to do this type of shitty work."

"The ladder may not hold me. You are lighter"

"It's your goddamned house, you go first."

Tyler knew from the look on her face and her cussing that she was on her game, on construction mode. He knew he'd have to go first.

The ladder looked sturdy—125 years could have weakened it. He used the broom and brushed away the cobwebs. Shining one of the lamps into the hole, he saw the ladder went down about six feet onto a dirt floor. He turned and started to descend. The ladder held and was really quite sturdy. He shook each rung to make sure his ascent would not be compromised. He asked Serena to get a rope in case they needed it to get back up. She did. Once at the bottom, he turned and shined the light on the space. Serena tied off the rope on one of the swivels on the fireplace and yelled down to him.

He said "Come down slowly. The ladder will hold, but I'm not sure for how long." He helped her down, boosting her butt of course, and they both laughed.

"Just needed to make sure you didn't fall."

"I'm sorry I yelled at you up there," she said. They kissed and looked around.

CHAPTER TWENTY-SIX

The floor was all dirt. The room was about six feet wide and was as long as the front of the house to the other end of the fireplace, probably forty feet in all. The walls were the stone that made up the foundation, on all sides. The room was attached to the basement, but you wouldn't be able to tell there was another room while standing in the basement. Toward the front of the house there were four cots lined up parallel to the walls. They still had blankets and small pillows on them. In the middle, there was a small table with candles and some eating utensils and metal plates and cups. On the far right, past the ladder at the end of the fireplace, was a small bookshelf that had a bible on it. The halogen lamps lit up the room like daylight. The fireplace had a small firebox in it, which was the origin of the hole in the upstairs fireplace. Above the bookcase a large root protruded from the wall and was surrounded by a crumbling foundation.

"Look at that," Tyler said. "The root from that giant oak grew right through the wall over the years. You know what this is, Serena? It's the room where they hid the runaways. This was a depot for the Underground Railroad. They were able to have a fire down here because the smoke mingled with the smoke from the kitchen fireplace. It wouldn't be noticed. Pia was right."

They marveled as they looked around some more. Tyler was looking at the cots and Serena was looking at the bible when she looked up and said "Tyler, look at this." He went over and they both looked at the root sticking out. She moved a light closer.

"That wall is open behind the root. The floor is littered with stone but there is no dirt," she said. "Dirt should have poured through here." She pulled away another stone and shone a light into the gap. There was another wall about four feet behind the root. They moved the bookcase and started to take away some of the stone blocks. There was another small room there. Careful not to cause any cave in's, they took stones out one by one until the room came into view. They saw a canvas covering something on the floor. They removed most of the rest of the wall until the alcove was open. Tyler shined the light on the pile and Serena removed the canvas. They both stared, mouths open, and couldn't believe what they saw. Before them was a pile of gold bars, counting 5 across and 5 wide, 2 layers total.

"Holy shit. Is this gold? Is this really gold?" Serena blurted out.

Tyler scampered up the ladder, up to the spare bedroom and grabbed his metal detector. He was down in thirty seconds flat. It turned on, he set a couple of dials, and the detector started going crazy as he pointed it. When they got back their composure, they looked at the bars.

"Look at these bars here," Tyler noted. "These five have South Carolina embossed on them. They moved some around and mentally recorded twenty five bars with five different states embossed on them, and the other twenty five more crudely shaped bars had no etching on them.

"Tyler, what is this? Where did this come from?" Serena asked in amazement.

"I have no clue. We have to find out," Tyler answered.

They sat there and talked giddily for about a half hour, trying to decide what it was, what to do, and how much it was all worth. Serena grabbed her phone and took videos of the room and the small chamber that held the gold. Tyler had done some quick math — there was over $30 million in gold sitting right in front of them.

"Maybe we should get Charlie over here. He may know what we should do," Tyler suggested.

They were both just sitting there laughing and still somewhat in shock. Then Serena looked at Tyler and said "Have you ever fucked on a pile of gold?"

Tyler responded," No, but I like the way you think."

So, they did. And they laughed the whole time, trying to figure out who was going to lay their back on the gold. It was cold. Tyler lost, of course.

CHAPTER TWENTY-SEVEN

C harlie said "Serena, it's 9PM. I'm not coming over there now. I'll be there in the morning.

"Charlie Washington, I am more serious than I ever have been in my life. You get your ass over here right now. This cannot wait!" Serena ordered. He finally agreed to be over in 20 minutes. Serena heard him mumbling as he hung up, "Damn women."

When Charlie got there, they went through the whole process again, opening the panel. Serena videoed the whole thing. As soon as he went down the ladder he said "This was the Underground Railroad. I cannot believe my eyes."

Tyler walked him over to the alcove and said "If you cannot believe that, then what do you make of this," as he threw back the canvas covering the gold.

Charlie's legs almost buckled. Serena had to catch him. "*Oh, my word*," and he whistled at the gold. "Is it real?"

Tyler answered, "According to my metal detector it is. I set it on heavy metal and it screamed at us."

Charlie was speechless for a couple of minutes. Then he said, choked up, "Pia was right. My great, great, Grandaddy was hung over this. Remember her words, Tyler? 'Where is it? Where did you hide it, boy?' Then they hung him. He knew this was down here. But he wouldn't let it go. He wanted it for his family. We need to talk to Pia. But first, we need to call the sheriff."

Serena said "The sheriff? Why the sheriff?"

Tyler said "He's right. I learned this in college and during my metal-detecting days. This is considered buried treasure and, by law, you have to inform the authorities of the find, even if it is yours to keep."

"Do you care if I call Sandra?" Charlie asked.

"Please call and have her come over. If the sheriff comes over, he'll bring the 5th army with him. She needs to see this before everyone else gets here," Tyler answered, anticipating the chaos that was coming.

Charlie had made it there in twenty minutes. Hearing the urgency in his voice, Sandra was there in about seven minutes. They went through everything with her and when she saw the room, she almost started crying. When she saw the gold she almost fainted.

The sheriff, Steve Morris, an old friend of Charlie's, came and looked at Charlie and said, 'Charlie, given the normal color of your skin, I believe you are pale. What happened? Why am I here at 10PM?"

They walked through all of it one more time, this time for the sheriff. Charlie went out to his truck and got some tools to nail the ladder completely secure. With so many people going up and down, he didn't want any accidents.

The sheriff was amazed at it all. Back upstairs, he looked at Tyler and said, "You know, the gold is one thing. But the underground railroad room is something that is altogether different. It is history right here. I think I have more appreciation for that room than the gold. Well, maybe. That is a lot of gold! I am going to post two deputies outside for the night with no knowledge of why they are there. No one is to get through other than you four. And in the early morning, I will send an armored truck in to pick up the gold. I'll set it up tonight. The deputies will help load it and then escort it to the bank. I'll call the bank president tonight to let him know of a deposit that will be made in the AM." He looked at all four of them while he said "Not a word to anyone until this gold is locked in the bank vault. I am going to have it moved to the Federal Reserve bank in Richmond later tomorrow. When word gets out, I don't want that gold in my county."

They all nodded in agreement. Charlie said "The only person we have to tell is Auntie Pia. She has to know."

The sheriff said "Sure. If anyone deserves to know this, it is her. Besides, if I said no, she would tongue lash me forever. She is the only woman, other than my mother, that intimidates me.

Charlie said, "What about Betty, your wife of 30 years?"

The Sheriff answered, "She don't scare me."

Sandra guffawed and said "You lie like a dog, Steven. You really are a politician."

The sheriff looked at Tyler and said "Tyler, you need to do some quick research on treasure law and how it is interpreted. I don't have much experience, but I do know every now and then an artifact will surface along these rivers and sometimes there could be legal ramifications. You might think of getting a lawyer. Just a bit of advice from a friend." With those words, he said his goodnights and left.

"I'm going to spend the night here with Tyler to make sure he is ok," Charlie offered, but Serena interrupted, "No need, Charlie. I have clothes in the truck. I'll stay. And you're right. He doesn't need to be alone tonight."

Tyler looked at Sandra and said, "I guess I don't have a say in this."

And Serena shot back "No, you don't."

Charlie shook his head. "There he goes, the rabbit in his hutch. And what about you, Missy? Clothes in your truck?"

"Charlie Washington, I know she is like your daughter. But this is none of your business," Sandra interjected. "Shut up! Let's go."

And Serena added, "Yea, Charlie, shut the hell up," and winked at Sandra. Sandra said "One more thing; as soon as the deputies leave tomorrow, I'll call you and we'll go see Aunt Pia. I cannot wait to show her this video."

Serena said "I can't either. She will be beside herself."

Sandra and Charlie left and, within five minutes, a deputy car was at the end of the drive. Both of them felt better with them outside.

Serena said "I need a bath badly after the cobwebs and the dust. Care to join me? Just a bath, really."

"No," Tyler said. "You take your bath and then I'll take mine. While you're up there I'll make us a snack. All of this treasure hunting has made me hungry. And, I'm worn out. You are like the Eveready bunny. I need to work up to your caliber."

She replied "It comes with the territory. You better keep up with me, mister. We *both* have some catching up to do."

CHAPTER TWENTY-EIGHT

Tyler and Serena were both up early the next morning, cleaned up and ready for the day. At 7AM, Tyler received a call on his cell from the sheriff and was told the armored car was two minutes out. He looked outside and he saw the deputies coming up the steps to the porch, a male and a female deputy. Introductions were made and he welcomed them and offered coffee, which they gladly accepted.

One deputy asked, "What's going on here?"

Serena came into the kitchen and said "Hey, Johnny."

Johnny looked up, looked at her, looked at Tyler, looked back at Serena, and said "Somebody has *finally* tamed you. Good for you, Tyler!"

Serena said, "Fuck you, Johnny," and they all laughed. Serena said "Johnny and I went to school together and ran around together for a while. Sophomore year he was in love with Barbara and I was his go-between."

Johnny said "I've been married 15 years, with kids, but every time my wife and I see Barbara and Craig, she reminds us all how I was in love with her when I was 15. She is a real piece of work."

Tyler said, "I just met her a month or so ago and I couldn't agree more with you."

Tyler continued "In about two minutes you are going to see something the likes of which you probably will never see again. Sheriff Morris has sworn us all to secrecy, until tomorrow morning. Are the both of you ok with that?"

They both nodded their agreement. Deputy Johnny said "This really must be something, for the sheriff to have talked to you and the orders we were given, which is what you just said. Trust us. We have seen a lot of stuff in our tenure. And it doesn't look like this is going to be a crime scene at all."

The armored guys came and Tyler took them through the whole process again of how he found the door. Eight new eyes looked at the pile of gold and just stood there for a good two minutes. One of the armored car guys was African American and, after his initial shock, looked around the room and kept very quiet, looking at the cots, the table, and down at the bible on the bookcase. Tyler went up to him, put his hand on his shoulder, and they just stood there in silence for a couple of minutes. Tyler said, "I know. This is a bigger treasure than the gold." The man looked up and nodded agreement. The statement was prophetic, but Tyer didn't know it at the time.

The decision was made to start a moving chain where the bars would be passed along. Tyler was taller than any of them, so he lifted the bars, moved them to the ladder, Johnny received them, and the other four moved them to the truck, which was backed up to the bottom of the porch steps. Within a half hour, they were done. Tyler came up rubbing his arms. Fifty gold bars at twenty pounds each was a real workout. He would be sore for a couple of days.

The guy from the armored car received a phone call. So did the other deputy. They both hung up and informed the group there were new plans. The deputies would escort the truck to route 17, where the state police would take up the escort. They were going straight to the Federal Reserve in Richmond, no stops. At the Virginia line, Federal Marshalls would meet the truck and finish the escort. Tyler thought, 'Wow, this is a big deal.' Once again, he didn't know how prophetic this statement would turn out to be.

CHAPTER TWENTY-NINE

Charlie and Sandra went over to Aunt Pia's to get her ready and let her know she was about to have company. They wouldn't tell her what was going on. And, of course, she complained the entire time while getting dressed about all the secrecy. It was about 9:30 when a knock came at the door. Barbara and Janice came in and asked what was going on. Sandra made them all coffee and, about ten minutes later, Serena and Tyler came in.

Serena said "Sorry we're late. I had to stop at my house for something. Aunt Pia looked at them both, then looked at Sandra, who had a big smile on her face.

"Lordy, Lordy," She started, getting misty eyed. "If I have to say so myself, looking at the two of you together makes my heart glad. As the bible would put it, the two of you were in the wilderness and finally found your way."

Serena reached down and gave her a big hug and kiss.

"Yes, we have, Aunt Pia."

"They found their way alright," Charlie said.

All of the women at the same time started scolding Charlie.

Then Pia asked, "What's this all about?"

Barbara added "Yes, what's this all about? Something big I hope, since I ducked out of work."

While everyone was talking, Tyler had been hooking up an HD cable to the back of the TV. He finally completed it and plugged Serena's phone into a special jack for a phone connection to the big screen.

Pia said, "Tyler, you better not have messed up that TV. I don't know it so well and my story comes on at 11AM."

Tyler began the oration of the story. He began by saying he was cleaning and repairing the fireplace in the kitchen. The video started and lasted a good five to six minutes, and everyone was silent and dumbfounded throughout the entire viewing. At the end, as the gold was shown, the video clicked pause, with the gold on the screen.

Barbara jumped up and blurted "We were standing right over that room the other night. All of us, standing right over it. Who would have ever known?"

Janice just sat there with her mouth open and Pia was again misty eyed. Sandra and Serena went over on both sides of Pia's chair, consoling her. Tears started streaming down her face and it took her about five minutes to compose herself.

"Charlie," Pia started again and said, "Your great, great, grand-daddy was hung over a pile of gold. Those were his last words, remember Charlie. 'Where is it, boy. Where you hiding it?' That meant that Zack knew the gold was here."

Tyler said "But he told those men 'I don't know, he died'. I would assume he was talking about Virgil, correct?"

"Yes, he was talking about Virgil," Pia continued. "My grand-daddy knew that his daddy had secrets with Virgil. And, he told me, years later before his Mama Sarah died, she told him the same. And, Sarah said she would go to her grave with those secrets, because her husband was hung over it. She would not let that happen to her children. Those were his words as he told me."

There was a lull in the conversation while all of them processed this information. Barbara finally said, "I am really lost. Someone please explain what this is all about."

"I'll catch you up," Tyler said. "Just give us a minute. Aunt Pia, I forgot to take that picture with me the other day. Is it still here?"

Pia reached under the coffee table and handed it to Tyler. Tyler gave it to Barbara and said "That is my great, great, great, grandmother, Phoebe Thorne. G3, right, Aunt Pia?"

Aunt Pia said, "See Charlie, Tyler gets it."

Barbara and Janice looked at the picture, and Barbara, never for a loss of words, looked at Tyler, back at the picture, and again at Tyler and said *"Oh My Lanta.* You are a spitting image, especially your eyes!"

Serena took the picture and just nodded her head. She said "Tyler, you told me you looked like Phoebe. But this is remarkable, that many generations ago."

Janice said "How much gold do you think there is? I mean, any ideas of the total worth?"

Charlie said "First of all, the gold is on its way to the Federal Reserve Bank in Richmond, as we speak. It is gone, which is why we showed you the video of it. From some quick calculations Tyler and I did, there is probably in excess of $36 million in that pile," pointing to the TV screen and the pile of gold showing.

Janice chimed in "I know I'm not the sharpest knife in the drawer. But, knowing my friend here (pointing at Barbara), word is going to get out pretty quickly. You might want to get the Chowan Herald involved so there are no misconceptions as to the whereabouts of the gold."

Barbara said, "And deprive me of the opportunity to break this story?"

Tyler said, "She's absolutely right."

Barbara said "I'll take care of it with you, Tyler. I know the editor, and she might think she'll get a Pulitzer for this, or something. She will print a special edition if she has to."

Tyler said "Thanks, Barbara. I appreciate it. We'll go this afternoon. Serena, you have to take me back to get my truck."

Aunt Pia said "My story comes on in 20 minutes. If you want to stay and watch it, fine. If not, it's time to shoo you all out." She looked directly at Tyler and said," Tyler, your fight is about to begin. Mark my words, that gold got my great granddaddy hung, and it is going to bring you trouble. Just remember what life is all about."

That statement scared Tyler. He knew first-hand what greed and avarice could do to people, given his recent experience with a woman he thought he loved and he thought loved him. He made a firm promise to himself not to let that happen here.

Chapter Thirty

As Tyler and Serena pulled into his driveway, they noticed a dark sedan parked on the side of the road, which followed them up the driveway. As they got out, the sedan pulled up behind them and a man and a woman got out, each holding up badges. The woman approached them and said "Tyler Harrington?"

Tyler replied "Yes. How can I help you?" looking at their badges.

"The woman said "I am Federal Marshall Janet Livingston and this is my partner Marshall Jake Butler. We escorted your cargo to Richmond and have been tasked with investigating this case. She looked at Serena and said "And you are?"

"Serena Milner," she answered. Tyler interjected, "She is my girlfriend."

Serena looked at Tyler with a grin and said, "I like the way you think."

Tyler said "Please come in. Can I offer you any coffee?" They both accepted and all four went into the house.

After Tyler served coffee, Marshall Livingston started.

"Mr. Harrington, the only background we have is that we escorted a load of gold in an armored car to Richmond that was found here. Taking the gold from North Carolina to Virginia made it an interstate transportation of found treasure. The FBI has waived any involvement since the Justice Department via the Federal Reserve is our jurisdiction. What we need is to file a report on the whole discovery. And please, the initial reaction from most people is that they are under suspicion for committing a crime. From what I've been told so far by your sheriff, this is not the case here. The more we find out, the better our report will be. On the phone, he told us a little bit about how you found it. And honestly, I am really intrigued by this whole event. And Miss Milner, the sheriff gave nothing but praise of your character."

Serena answered "I'll have to thank the sheriff for that. And, please, call me Serena."

They all got up and Tyler went through the whole thing again. In the underground room, Marshall Jake Butler whistled and said "This is something. This room is history itself. I wonder what the gold looked like sitting there."

Serena pulled out her phone and fast forwarded to the part where they uncovered the pile of gold. Marshall Livingston said "May we have a copy of that video? A video is worth a thousand words."

Upstairs, Serena typed in her cell number and forwarded the video to her.

Marshall Livingston then said, "Thank you both for your cooperation. I would offer some friendly advice. First, and from my experience, when word of this gets out, there will be a media circus on your property. I would contact the sheriff to have deputies posted here for about a week, until the novelty wears off. Second, hire a good attorney, one with experience in treasure hunting. We have both worked cases of found artifacts, found jewelry, and some buried loot. Again, with interstate transport of these items, it can get very, very nasty. We have both given testimony in court many times. And lastly, publish your story as soon as possible, so would-be thieves understand the gold is no longer here. It is important to be proactive rather than reactive. A good treasure attorney will know that."

Tyler said "As soon as you leave, I'm meeting a friend at the local newspaper to do just that. We are also going to release the video to them, so we won't be hounded by visitors to see the room. I have an attorney in Philadelphia who is not only my attorney, but also a friend. I can call him this afternoon. Thank you so much for the advice."

"One last thing," Tyler said. "If the justice department is involved with this, who will have ultimate jurisdiction over the actual gold?"

Marshall Butler said "Normally, the Federal Government. But some of that gold had state markings on it. There is going to be a fight, believe me."

The Marshalls gave them their cards with phone numbers, in case they needed to contact them with any other information. They said their goodbyes and left.

Tyler and Serena sat for a couple of minutes to process all that had happened. She sent the video to Tyler's phone to give to the newspaper.

Serena agreed to contact the sheriff mainly to thank him for the kind words. She would ask him to post a car at the entrance of the driveway, given they were going to publish the story that same day. Then she went to work. Tyler went to the newspaper office to meet Barbara.

At the newspaper office, he gave the video to the editor, who also took additional statements and partially wrote the headlines and story. She promised two things: there would be a special morning edition of the Chowan Herald to go out to all customers, with additional copies made for common distribution; and she promised to publish follow-ups to the story as they occurred. Secondly, she promised to file the story with the video immediately on the AP wire service. That way, TV stations could get hold of it and run the story. They agreed to make sure the hook of the story would be that the gold was now in the Federal Reserve vault in Richmond. The AP report was filed at 3PM that afternoon.

Tyler and Serena were sitting at his kitchen table having a glass of wine that evening, around 7PM, talking about the whole day. They heard cars and a commotion outside and looked out to see a CNN van blocking the street. There were at least a dozen people with still cameras and two TV cameras on top of vans.

Serena said softly "Holy Shit."

CHAPTER THIRTY-ONE

About ten minutes after watching the news story on the national news, Serena' phone rang. It was her brother on her phone. Five seconds later, Tyler's phone rang. It was Jerry. He started out by saying "Tyler, what the hell is going on? You found gold? The picture of you in your chef's coat is all over the news and the video is playing non-stop. It's all over the internet and has over four million hits already. You hit instant fame, buddy!"

"Take a breath, Jerry," Tyler answered.

"Kathy is still at work." Jerry continued. "Otherwise, she would have been all over you. She is with a client and one of her assistants interrupted an important meeting so they could all watch the 7PM news. She texted me to watch and to call you. As soon as she is out of her meeting, I know she'll call you. Get ready for it."

Tyler caught Jerry up with the pared down version, since he had already watched the video on the news, but he had to stop it short. "Uh Oh. Kathy is ringing in. I better talk to her." He hung up with Jerry, clicked the line, and said, "You need a loan?"

Kathy blurted "My God, Tyler. I leave you alone for a couple of months and all hell breaks loose. I am so happy for you. I couldn't believe what the TV was saying. I watched it again on the internet, and, *My God*. All of that gold. How much is it worth, really?"

"Cool your heels, sister. It's not a done deal. The news left out one bit of information that changes everything. Half of the gold bars have state markings on them, gold that came from six different states."

Kathy asked, "What does that mean?"

"It means," Tyler continued, "I have to get Maury involved. The gold will be tied up in court for a long time. Each state will claim their share. There is over $35 million in gold, half of which is accounted for. The other half isn't. I just happened to find it in a hidden basement in my cellar."

"You mean the underground railroad?" She asked

"Yes." Tyler continued. "It really is remarkable, more remarkable than the gold. There is a long story to it. I can't do it over the phone. I need to come up there and get with Maury."

I'll set it up and call you as soon as he gets back to me," Kathy answered.

"Kathy, one more thing," Tyler said. I have even bigger news than the gold." Serena had hung up with her brother and Tyler motioned her to come closer.

Kathy said, "I have *got* to hear this."

Tyler said, "I met someone."

They heard Kathy gasp.

He continued, "Do you remember that day we met in the bar."

She hesitantly said, "Yes. Is it one of those three ladies that watched you the whole time?"

Tyler said "Yes." Serena was almost laughing out loud. She had to hold it back. She knew what was coming.

Kathy said, "Is it the one with the long hair?"

Tyler said no.

Was it the one looking straight at you?

Tyler said no.

Kathy said "Tyler, the girl you watched walk the entire length of the bar is a lesbian. That's what you told me. So, which one is it?"

"I converted the lesbian" he said.

Kathy blurted "Bullshit, Tyler. Quit messing with me."

He laughed and said "Ok, Ok. Turns out she wasn't a lesbian; it was a cover to keep guys like me away from her."

Kathy interrupted and said "I can see why. You watched her butt the whole way across the bar," Serena laughed out loud.

"Oh God," Kathy moaned. "She's listening. You are such an ass, Tyler."

Tyler simply answered, 'Kathy, say hello to Serena." Serena yelled hello and Kathy said hello back.

Kathy said, "Tyler, even though you are an ass, I'm happy for you, you know that. When do I get to meet her?"

"Well, if I can get to see Maury, we'll come up this week. Can we make a reservation for your spare bedroom?" He looked at Serena for approval. She shook her head yes, she'd go.

Kathy happily obliged. "Just let me know so I can clear my schedule."

It was set. He'd call her back as soon as Maury called him.

They hung up and Tyler told the story of how Maury saved him from his ex-girlfriend and their partners. He said "Maury is very young, mid-thirties, short, a little funny-looking with frizzy hair, and talks real fast. He represents his clients and protects them like a tiger and is the sharpest lawyer I have ever met. That is why Kathy uses him. I met him through Kathy and her firm. He came to the restaurant to eat a couple of times and then one day he called me and said he was bringing this girl over that he was in love with and he really wanted to impress her. I knew him, but not really that well; just from a couple of Kathy's parties where we met, mingled and chatted. So that night, he brought this girl in and I put the show on for her. I even lit flambé at the table for dessert. They've been married now for about three years. He loves me. Said I was the last nail he needed to get them together. When he represented me, we became much closer, played racquetball, and went out a couple of times. He's a good guy."

A short time later, Maury called and set up a meeting for Thursday morning at 9AM. He saw the news after Kathy called him. The last thing he told Tyler was that if the gold came through unscathed, he was charging him through the nose. They laughed and hung up.

Then, Kathy called back and said there was a cookoff in downtown Philadelphia that weekend with Chefs from all over the world. She had entered Tyler's name and he had been accepted.

Tyler started to push back, but Kathy stopped him. "Tyler, you can do this in your sleep. Even though you are now in the south, you still have a name, and right now you are in the national spotlight. I am an opportunist, you aren't. Do your thing, then go home. It's that simple."

Again, Serena was listening and nodded her head and mouthed "Do it."

CHAPTER THIRTY-TWO

On Wednesday, they drove to Philadelphia. It was a 7-hour drive and they talked the entire trip. There was so much to talk about, given the events of the past several days, not to mention their hot-and-heavy physical relationship. They both agreed that they were on mental overload and the physical part helped with the stress.

At some point, Tyler said "There is something else I haven't told you yet. I went to visit Aunt Pia yesterday, of course, after her stories were over. She was on her laptop doing research. It is amazing the mental capacity she maintains for a 95-year-old woman. Anyway, it has been bothering me how my family basically disintegrated over the last two generations. If Phoebe Thorne was a shipping heiress, what happened to the shipping company? I posed that to Aunt Pia and she said there was only one way to find out. She made two phone calls to a friend of a friend and gave me the name of a 70-year-old librarian at the Free Library of Philadelphia. We have an appointment at 2PM tomorrow, after the meeting with Maury. Pia says the library may have articles from the Philadelphia Inquirer, from the mid-19th century up to today. We may be able to find articles regarding the shipping line my family owned. It has been bothering me why my grandmother never talked about it. Or my dad, for that matter. It just never came up and I didn't know any different."

They arrived in the late afternoon at Kathy and Jerry's house and were greeted by the whole family. Their two children immediately accosted Tyler and wanted him to play video games. Introductions were made and they all settled around the kitchen table. After five minutes of chatting, the kids badgered "Uncle" Tyler to play with them. So, he and Jerry took them to the family room to play.

Kathy started the conversation by saying "Tyler and I have known each other for a long time. He was hurt badly, Serena. I really didn't think he'd come out of it. But here you are. How did you do it? More so, how did you get him out of his funk?

Serena told the story about her issues and how she learned of his issues from the article, how they met, what happened at the truck, and some of the sparring they initially did. Her friend had told her he watched her walk the entire length of the bar that day. She said what really hooked him was the night of the fundraiser.

"What happened the night of the fundraiser?" Kathy asked with interest.

"Well, Tyler was doing his thing. He was incredible. It was an awesome evening and he became the toast of the town. Everyone wanted to meet him and he was really working the crowd. I knew then the talent he has. In a lull, he was looking at his phone and I walked up to him. You see, that night I was wearing my 'fuck me' dress."

Kathy blurted *"Oh-no-you-didn't?* I have a couple of those dresses and Jerry forbids me to wear them. What happened?"

"He thought he was cool, after he put his tongue back in his mouth," she said. "I knew to go slow but I also knew he would come around. We met a couple of times at the bar after that. Then he asked me out on New Year's Eve. That was it."

"One more thing," Serena continued. "Is there a remote chance that his ex will be there Saturday night?"

Kathy responded honestly, "If she is, she better not show her face. I'll tear her throat out. Why do you ask?"

Serena answered, "Well, I bought another dress on Monday."

Kathy said "Screw Jerry, I'll wear one too, just in case. It's going to be fun, trust me."

Tyler, in between the beeps and the boops of the video game, heard Kathy and Serena talking non-stop, laughing, and then talking in low tones. He knew Kathy was working Serena and vice-versa. Kathy was very outspoken and he knew Serena could hold her own. They were definitely bonding, and quickly. Then the thought occurred to him what Charlie had said about 'having to deal with the women in your life.' It became apparent to him all of a sudden and he had a new appreciation for Charlie; and Jerry sitting across from him.

Of course, Kathy made Tyler cook dinner that night. They opened some wine and everyone pitched in. Serena thought to herself— *After two totally different relationships than this one, this relationship is how it is supposed to be.* Or, did she find a guy that had the same interests as her, was extremely social, and made her feel like she was the only reason he existed. He wasn't trying to make it happen. It was natural. She could see spending the rest of her life with him. It scared her. She was all in, again. But *screw it.* It was all or nothing and she felt confident Tyler felt the same way. If his ex-girlfriend did show up, she might beat Kathy to the punch.

After a wonderful evening, Kathy took them to their room, gave them towels and whatever else they might need, and said, "Tyler, you know what you are going to make Saturday night?"

"Tyler said "I think so."

"Let me know what you need and, between Jerry and I, we'll take care of it."

Tyler said "Thanks. I think I'll be ok. I may hit that farmer's market I saw on the way in and see what they have. Farm to fork, you know."

Kathy laughed. "I got it. No matter, I got you into this. We're here for you. And, remember. There are kids in the house. Don't make me split you two up."

Tyler said "OK, Charlie." Serena laughed and just waved Kathy off with a never-mind shrug.

They said their goodnights. Both of them were exhausted. They got into bed and fell asleep immediately.

Chapter Thirty-Three

At 9AM the next morning they were both sitting across the desk from Maury Greenbaum. Tyler introduced Serena to Maury and, of course, Maury told the story of how Tyler was responsible for him getting married. Tyler was right. He was a genuinely nice guy. A little young, but nonetheless capable. Then he got right to it.

"For the last couple of days, I have been researching your issue in the evenings. It involves much more than I am proficient in. I contacted James Dodson, an attorney in Raleigh who, being close, knew about your discovery and agreed to come on board as co-counsel. His specialty has been in recovered artifacts, treasure, and any other lost historical items found. He said it is incredible the number of items found each year that treasure hunters find on and around the coast. Litigation is hot and heavy when something is found, especially if it is not cut and dry where it was found, and who lost it. He will work for me and will go along with whatever financial structure you and I come up with. I'll get to that part later."

Tyler looked at Serena and said "I told you there is a lot out there." She just nodded.

"What he told me was what I thought would happen. First,

each state will sue you for their claim on the gold. They will pull no stops for recovery. And, they will all get together and claim the remainder of the gold that is unmarked, as part of the same hoard; his term, not mine. I contacted the Chowan County Courthouse and verified that if any suits were brought regarding the gold, hearings would be held there, not in any other county or state, since the gold was found there. This could get ugly quickly. I just want you to know up front what you will be up against."

Tyler took it all in and remarked "Maury, I am going to fight this as long as I can. That gold was hidden there for a reason and a man was hung over it. I have to play it out as far as I can."

Maury then said "Just so you know, I normally would charge by the hour. In this case, it could also be a percentage, given the amount of money involved. However, you paid me well in the last case and, as a friend, I really think you might walk out of this with nothing. Those sharks in each state will be out for blood. If they eat you, then they'll start eating each other."

He looked at Serena and said, "Welcome to my world."

Tyler asked, "How do we make this arrangement then?"

Maury said "We'll do it on billable hours for now, for both me and Mr. Dobson. I will give you weekly updates on the case and on the billed hours. That way, you'll get a feel for how much it will cost in the long run. Trust me, Tyler. I will only bill you enough to cover my costs and a little profit. I am doing this for you as a friend and someone I care about. That woman screwed you over royally, personally and financially, and I will never get over it. It was a damn shame; but this will probably cost you anywhere from $30 to $50 thousand up front."

Serena blurted, "Holy shit!"

Maury said, "Holy shit is right. And Tyler, now for the really bad news."

Tyler said "What else can they possibly want?"

"When I called the courthouse, the clerk there said a cease-and-desist order was being filed on behalf of the North Carolina Preservation Society, the NAACP, the American Heritage Society, and a couple more. You cannot touch your house until all information given to these associations is provided and reviewed."

Serena said "I've dealt with these people in the past. They all mean well and have everyone's best interest at heart, except for the owner of the property. Things can get a little tricky and usually lawyers need to get involved."

Maury said "Exactly, not a real big deal, but a huge nuisance in the long run."

Tyler said firmly "That is my house and my heritage. I will fight for that and spend a lot more money for my house before I'll fight for the gold. Listen to me, Maury. Under no circumstances will I waver on that house."

Maury said "Understood."

They said their goodbyes and Tyler thanked him at least six more times. Maury said he'd be in touch with dates, and planning, as it could take several months before anything happened.

On the way out, Serena looked at Tyler and said "How are you going to manage all of this? I mean, financially. This could bankrupt you."

"It won't bankrupt me, but it could put a big damper on the remodeling project." May take years to get the house and property the way I want it."

They drove to the library and met Josephine Bartkowski the librarian Pia had set up for them to meet. Because of Aunt Pia's reputation, Mrs. Bartkowski had already pulled most of the information they needed. She had pulled articles from the early 1900's and, sure enough, the information was there. Tyler typed on his laptop while Serena dictated. When they were done, he emailed Aunt Pia and Sandra.

"I'm sure we'll have many conversations about this when we get back," Tyler commented.

What they learned was that the Williams Shipping Line was established in, or around, 1750 as a whaling company, and later moved into cargo and the transportation of goods. In 1917, during the height of the U-boat war in the Atlantic Ocean, Williams Shipping lost 18 of their 22 ships to torpedoes. The government contract and the insurance money were barely enough to cover the loss of ships, and the company made the decision to compensate all families of the merchant seamen that were lost. Tyler Thorne Jr. sold the remaining assets and Williams Shipping folded after 165 years of business.

"That's about the time my grandmother was born," Tyler explained. She never knew what happened or what that lifestyle was like. No wonder she never talked about it."

CHAPTER THIRTY-FOUR

Tyler worked all day Friday on his presentation and what he was going to prepare. That afternoon, he and Serena went to a local farm market and purchased all of the ingredients he would need. Early Saturday morning, they took all of the produce and delivered it to the competition hotel, and worked on the set-up. He figured he was ready. They left to rest for a while and planned to come back for the event in the afternoon.

All Tyler had to do was shower, shave, and put on his chef's smock and nice slacks. When Serena came down, he was floored. He said "My god, it's another..." But Serena cut him off. She pointed to the kids and the babysitter. Jerry came in looking good wearing a nice suit, saw Serena, and said "Oh, *shit*."

They both looked at him quizzically. Then Kathy came in and Tyler said "Wow. 'Oh, shit' is right, Jerry. You both look amazing. What's going on?"

Kathy looked at him grinning and said, "Just in case some unwelcome visitor decides to show up."

Tyler looked at Serena, who did a semi-twirl and asked, "You Like?"

"Both of you, put your tongues back in your mouth and let's go," Kathy said jokingly.

"We're not wasting that dress tonight, you know," Jerry warned. Kathy just smiled.

On the way, Tyler admonished both of them regarding the reason they both had decided to dress up. He had hoped he would never have to see Jill again and warned them that, if she did show up, they were both forbidden to make a scene.

"With Serena's body, Jill wouldn't dare approach you," Kathy said with conviction.

Serena added "I promise I won't leave your side tonight."

They checked their coats and entered the ballroom as people were just starting to arrive. There were several chefs in a group talking and, as they approached the group, one chef turned, Tyler stopped, and they both threw their arms around each other.

"Lui, I can't believe you are here. Why didn't you call me?"

Lui said, "I wanted to surprise you. Your friend Kathy set it all up."

Tyler and Lui turned to the others as they approached. Tyler began with the introductions. Luigi Posata, this is Jerry and Kathy Gilson."

As they were shaking hands, Luigi said "Kathy, good to finally meet you. And thank you for getting this bum to this event," kissing her on both cheeks. He shook hands with Jerry. Then Tyler said, "And this is Serena, my girlfriend."

Luigi looked at Tyler, then looked at Serena again and said "Madonna Mia. Che Bella Donna," while he kissed her on both cheeks.

Tyler answered in Italian, "Si, e bellissima dentro (Yes, she is beautiful inside)."

"That's enough of the Italian." Kathy interrupted. "I don't trust either one of you."

Serena, who was a little in shock, looked at Tyler and said, "You speak Italian?"

Tyler said, "Luigi and I were roommates for almost two years. We had school for eight months in Paris, where we became roommates and learned French. Then, we spent eight months in Rome together, and finally eight months in New York together. We basically had two years of the same schooling."

Luigi looked at Serena and said "He's not attractive, he can't cook, and he's not Italian. Serena, why is such a beautiful woman like you with a bum like this? Ah, I know. It is the gazillion dollars in gold he found. He is a bum, you know."

Tyler said laughing, "Stop that. As a matter of fact, we both found it, together."

"Seriously, I landed in America and all over the newspaper is your picture and stories about the gold," Luigi said. "Then Kathy called the event coordinator, and I was made aware she was trying to get you in."

Kathy added "I read Luigi was going to attend and I knew you two were thick as thieves. So, I started making phone calls. Just so you know, Luigi, I was having a hard time convincing the panel at such a late date to let Tyler in. Thank you for your intervention."

Luigi said grinning, "Any time I have the opportunity to kick his butt in a competition, I don't pass it up."

They all laughed.

Just then, a woman approached the group and Luigi announced—

"Ah, my wife Catarina."

He introduced her to everyone. She looked at Tyler and said, "Luigi has been going on about Tyler this, and Tyler that, all week. I am so glad to meet you. May I please join all of you for the event? I know no one here."

They all welcomed her graciously. Kathy looked at Serena and they grinned. Catarina was dressed like a typical Italian woman, oozing fashion. She looked like a model. She would be a great addition to the table.

Luigi and Tyler excused themselves to go into the anteroom to get ready. On the way, Luigi said "Tyler," biting his fist. Tyler said "Stop it. I think I'm in love," at which Luigi replied "Not bad, for you at least. What do you think of my Catarina?"

"Way out of your league," Tyler responded.

The evening was a big success. Luigi actually won the competition and Tyler came in third. They were all sitting around the table talking when Tyler said, "Stop, Luigi. I've cooked once in the last six months. I was out of practice. I knew you would beat me. I also knew we'd beat the rest of these people. I'm upset that girl came in second. My dessert screwed me."

"I know. But that Sweet Potato fritter was incredible," Luigi agreed. "How did you come up with that? Was that nutmeg in it?"

Tyler said, "No, a pinch of cinnamon, and cilantro."

Luigi continued, "Ahh. Really, it was good, the type of recipe that comes along only so often. How did you come up with it?

Tyler said, "Well, you know I worked with the recipe and..."

Serena interrupted Tyler and blurted, "That is Aunt Pia's recipe. I've eaten those a million times."

Luigi looked at a grinning Tyler and said "Busted!"

Just then, another chef and a nicely dressed gentleman walked to the table and excused themselves and asked Luigi for a word. A few moments later, Luigi asked Tyler to join the small meeting. After about ten minutes, while walking back to the table, Luigi was shaking Tyler's shoulders all excited.

Luigi said "Those two gentlemen are from a huge food conglomerate and they want us to represent their company's products in a big, international event in Bern, Switzerland, in three weeks. All expenses are paid. They asked me to put together a team of three and were pleased I chose Tyler immediately." He looked at Catarina, "I think Paolo might enjoy this also."

Catarina said "Oh, he is perfect." She looked at the others and said "Paolo grew up with us and is currently running the kitchen of a 5-Star Hotel in Rome. He has 1 Michelin Star."

Tyler said "There is only one condition for me to participate. Serena, you have to come with me. I won't go without you."

Luigi said "We'll practice in Pescara for a week and then drive to Bern." Catarina chimed in, "I will be your translator and tour guide while they are working. It will be fabulous. You'll love Pescara. You have to come."

"Serena, if you don't go, I will," Kathy threatened.

Finally, Serena looked at Tyler and said "I guess Charlie will have to watch over my crew and the courthouse. If you really want me to go, then I'm in."

Tyler smiled a wide smile, "Of course I want you to go."

"One thing, Serena," Luigi warned. "I know Italian men. Don't bring that dress with you." Catarina smacked him playfully and they all laughed.

If Jill was there, she never showed her face.

CHAPTER THIRTY-FIVE

The next few weeks were a whirlwind. Barbara and Janice were beside themselves, as their friend was going to Europe without them. None of them had really traveled to many places, let alone Europe. They took Serena shopping in Raleigh, forced her to buy new clothes, makeup, luggage, and anything else Serena really had never had a need for. Serena's brothers and their wives and kids made trips into town to meet this new guy they didn't know. Of course, Sandra was right in the middle of all of it. Charlie and Billy gave their word they'd take care of her business while she was gone.

The first week in Pescara was fabulous. The Posata house was right on the Adriatic Sea and the views were breathtaking. The boys worked during the day while the women shopped and went sightseeing. Catarina introduced Serena to Montepulciano wine from the Abruzzo region. Every household in Italy, it seems, has grapevines in their back gardens. They grow the grapes, make the wine, and never think twice about the quality or trying to impress anyone. It was a way of life, similar to how backyards in America have tomatoes growing in their gardens. Everyone has them. All of the wine was good. They also toured wineries that were hundreds of years old. It gave Serena a new appreciation for wine, one which she had not been exposed to prior to seeing the age and size of the oak barrels used. She was determined to learn about and appreciate wine differently than she had in the past, rather than just drinking it.

The shopping was fantastic and Serena was introduced to fashion; some aspects she was aware of, but others were entirely new to her. The emphasis on subtle accessories is what Italians are known for, and Serena fell right in with Catarina, her new style guru. The gold and jewelry was much less expensive in Italy, and Serena had to add up how many more jobs she'd need to work for some of the items she was buying.

The Apennine Mountains were an hour away and were incredible. Catarina had said driving the roads in a convertible was the only way to go. But it was winter and the higher they went, the colder it became. They kept the top up. The idea of building roads on mountains, and through mountains, was mind boggling to Serena. The views were nothing less than spectacular.

In the evenings, they made dinner, drank wine, and had many visitors stopping in. Word got out that Chef Luigi and Chef Paolo were working locally and all of their friends and relatives knew the food would be flowing. Dinners usually lasted until midnight. And, believe it or not, Serena picked up some Italian. It was hard to understand that she only knew one language, yet most Europeans knew English, as well as several other languages. The social aspect of Europe was what she was used to. Pescara is a big city. However, everyone knew everyone and was as social as her group was in North Carolina.

Pescara was intoxicating to both Tyler and Serena. They fell in love with the region, the people, and mainly the lifestyle. Tyler had mentioned to Serena, at one point, how the culture in Italy and other parts of Europe is more social, more interactive than it is in America. People congregate, socialize, and enjoy the company of their families and friends. In America, the work ethic and accumulation of goods and wealth takes precedence over all else, and the lifestyle becomes a grind, so much so that the little enjoyments of life are overlooked and become secondary in nature. Serena responded by saying that she had a new appreciation for her family and the group of friends they had; she wouldn't let material endeavors supersede those relationships. They both were in agreement. They knew someday they would return to 'Bella Pescara!'

The Posata team won the event in Bern. The winning factor was a sweet potato fritter that all of the judges agreed was a new and fresh take on the 'Farm to Fork' concept. The PR was incredible, and Tyler knew Kathy would go crazy. Pictures, write-ups, and interviews lasted well into the evening. Serena texted everyone constantly and sent pictures when the winning team posed on stage. Sandra sent a picture back of Aunt Pia giving the thumbs-up sign. She showed Tyler, Luigi, and Paolo the picture, and they all wanted it as a keepsake. She texted the Chowan Herald with a quick synopsis of the event and the picture of the winning team. She knew it would make the front page on that week's edition. Lastly, Serena called Kathy and they talked about the event for half an hour.

They flew back to Raleigh the next day, toting two extra suitcases Serena had to buy to hold all of the gifts she had brought back with her. They were exhausted. But Barbara forced them to show up at Millie's once they arrived in town. Serena was wearing a new outfit Catarina had helped her pick out and the women went crazy over her when she walked into Millie's. She was blushing and smiling from ear to ear. Tyler just loved watching Serena. *What a woman*, he thought.

They all convened at Charlie and Sandra's house, and Serena passed out all of her gifts. Tyler and Charlie just watched, sipping scotch. Charlie looked at Tyler and said "I don't think I have ever seen her shine like that."

"Charlie," Tyler said. "I was amazed at how a small-town girl like Serena held her own with the Italian women and other European women in Bern. They could not believe she owns a construction company. Serena is amazing and I count my blessings every day to be with her."

"You two rest tomorrow, jet lag and all," Charlie offered. "I'll take care of the courthouse, which, by the way, is almost finished. We do have to review the cease-and-desist order."

"I know," Tyler answered. "I talked to Maury this morning at the airport. He's coming down this week to see everything for himself."

Charlie said "Ok. Aunt Pia was busy while you were gone. She has some news for you. Of course, she won't tell me. You'll have to see her the day after tomorrow."

Tyler and Serena got into bed that night, smiled at each other once, and slept for almost ten hours.

CHAPTER THIRTY-SIX

The following day, Serena was super busy finishing up the courthouse project, and Tyler tried to figure out how far he could get around the cease-and-desist order. The yard always needed work. So, he busied himself with it.

Maury showed up Friday afternoon and Tyler took him through the fireplace, down into the room, and showed him where the gold was. After about ten times giving that tour, Tyler told Maury he could be a professional guide.

Of course, they went to Millie's around 6PM and were still the topic of conversation. Tyler took his customary ribbing for his win, but everyone was still impressed with it all. Maury was introduced and took a bunch of grief right off the bat, a big city lawyer and all. Fifteen minutes later, Serena came in wearing jeans and her work boots, as usual, and took a bunch of grief for her attire, and not being the cosmopolitan Serena that had come in the other night.

Tyler and Maury were sitting in a booth alone at one point and Maury said "You have fallen into a good crowd here. I can tell they like you and you like them. One question: How are you going to react when the big city urge hits? I know you are very content now. But face it, you were born and bred in the city, just like me."

Tyler thought a minute and said "Maury, the big city holds great memories for me. It also holds personal hurt that I don't know I'll ever get over. These people here are real. They don't put on fronts, they can't. Everyone knows everyone and knows everyone else's business. I thought that was intimidating at first. But there is a love that goes with it. They take care of their own and protect their own. Besides, Luigi and Paolo want me to be their third on our international competition team. We did well and will probably enter five or six competitions a year. That will keep me busy and provide some income if we do well. After the sponsorship cut, we each made about $10,000 per man in Bern. Of course, it is going right into the Maury Greenbaum legal fund."

Maury clinked Tyler's glass and said "It's a start. And you know how I like good starts. We'll talk later about the case. Right now, I want to talk to the ladies. You can get all the information you want if you just schmooze the ladies."

"Well, go to Barbara," Tyler suggested, "The lady right there, and start your schmoozing. She is a wealth of information and will not hesitate to pass it along. She's known as inter-Barbara, cousin to the internet. Make a comment on how good she looks after having two kids and she'll be putty in your hands."

Maury laughed and they went to mingle.

That evening, they were sipping wine in his kitchen as Tyler told him the story of the house and how he literally purchased a house his ancestors had built. He went through everything that happened, according to Aunt Pia. Maury interrupted him regarding Aunt Pia, and Tyler told him who she was and the relationship to his family, and everything she had related to him. Then he told him about the library and how she had done research and had set a meeting for him.

Then he talked about the house and described what he was going to do with it; how he would remodel the kitchen into a commercial kitchen that looked like any other non-commercial kitchen. Of course, he was keeping the fireplace as the showpiece. And he would actually keep it functional and use it.

"Barbara has a wealth of knowledge," Maury commented

during their conversation. "Not only did she anticipate what I was going to ask, she knows Judge Henry and all of his quirks and likes. She knows the State people and who will show up for the hearing. She didn't know James Dobson, but promised that she would 'get the skinny on him', which I think means she'll find out about his reputation. I thanked her and told her how nice she looked, and that I couldn't believe she had two kids."

"Then she puffed her chest out and said, 'even with two kids, I still have the perfect size and shape breasts. My husband considers them trophies.' How close am I?," Tyler ventured a guess.

Maury laughed, "You are dead on. What a piece of work she is."

"She is a piece of work," Tyler answered. "But she is very smart, very sociable, and has a heart of gold. She and Serena grew up best friends. And most importantly, her information is usually accurate. We need to use whatever she gives us."

Maury continued, after their glasses were refilled, "Let's talk about the hearing. It will be a media circus and each state will have at least three attorneys from their respective State Attorney General Offices. They will be heavy hitters and will try to intimidate us from the get-go with a show of force. The courtroom is going to be full of attorneys and spectators. It will be very intimidating. There will be me, you, and James Dobson at our table all by our lonesome."

He took a sip of wine and continued "Don't let them get to you. That gold has been there a long time. The bars stamped by each state will go to those states. I am almost convinced. According to James and treasure law, there is lost, mislaid, abandoned, embedded, and a treasure trove. I know it has been there 150 years and was found on your property. But if the original owners can be traced, they'll get it. And, previous owners of the property may come forth and claim it. You just don't know." [1]

He paused "The real question is about the gold with no markings and who it may belong to. The states will claim an equal share of that gold without proof of ownership. You have that same claim, depending on how the Judge interprets the law. If you win, each state will appeal. If they win, you have the right to appeal. North

Carolina may claim it solely over the other states, since it was found here. No matter what happens, Tyler, this can drag on for years and you could lose everything you have if you do not end up with the gold. And if you win, the taxes on treasure are just like any other income. You can lose up to 46% of it just in taxes."

"With taxes, they win no matter what," Tyler said in acknowledgement.

"The Federal Government does," Maury said. The state governments can be persuaded, depending on the circumstances."

The next morning, they met in the kitchen for coffee. Maury commented, "It was freezing last night. That space heater helped. But my nose is just now thawing. I'm going to take on the Historical Societies first thing Monday morning. You cannot live like this. I'll make sure the Department of Interior gets involved. They will supersede any one organization's claim over any other. Just promise not to touch that room and they may let you continue the remodeling. By the way, Tyler, this is a great house. My mother would love this place."

"Well, thank you. You know how I love Nora," Tyler answered. "Tell her she is officially invited when it is completed, as well as you and your bride."

CHAPTER THIRTY-SEVEN

The next day, Sunday, Tyler and Serena spent the whole day together. She convinced him to show her how to use the metal detector and they spent the cold afternoon walking through the woods around his house. They found some old nails, a couple of tin cans, and a horseshoe that may have been very old. Tyler explained carbon dating and how important it was for historical artifacts. He also explained the process of digging below the surface using the large detector to get a signal, and then using a small hand detector to pinpoint the item once dug up.

"The problem with some detector aficionados is where they look and what kind of damage they do to the property. Sometimes artifacts are two feet below the surface and they turn soil all over the place. I once saw the front lawn of a historical property that looked like a family of prairie dogs lived there. They had no consideration and left the property derelict. That is a big deal with most people who enjoy the hobby. Leave the property as you found it."

Serena enjoyed the metal detecting and the day. They promised each other to go near Albemarle Sound and do some investigating once the weather turned pleasant.

Even though the remodel was still at a standstill, Tyler kept busy all week. He was still working on the outside of the property. On

Tuesday, he was going to visit Aunt Pia and on Thursday he was asked to come into the culinary class at the high school to talk about his competition win in Bern, since it had made the front page of the paper. On Friday, he had a meeting with an architect to develop plans for his new detached garage and workshop. He was so impressed with Charlie's workshop he knew Serena would love to have one. He hired the architect to make sure it was the same design and material of the house.

Tyler worked all day Monday and Tuesday morning on the grounds. A little after noon, he made his way over to Aunt Pia's. She had lunch waiting for him and, when Charlie arrived, she said "I knew if I made lunch, you would show up."

You're right," Charlie said. "I knew you were making lunch."

"On behalf of me, Luigi, and Paolo, I'd like to present to you the first place medal we won in Bern," Tyler announced to Pia. He handed her a picture of the three of them on the stage, holding the medal. Around the outside of the frame was a ribbon holding the actual medal at the bottom of the picture. "If it wasn't for your recipe, we may not have won. So, we all wanted you to have this."

"I'll be damned," Charlie said. "She is actually speechless."

Aunt Pia started to tear up. She wiped her eyes and said, "Boy, put that on the mantle in front middle."

Charlie did and she thanked Tyler over and over. It was well known forever after. Anytime she had company, she would show off that picture and the medal.

Then she said "I've got something for you. You know, I may be old and my body is failing. But my mind is still working and I still know a lot of people, *a lot of people*! You take this to your lawyers and let them deal with it. I think it may help."

Tyler thanked her and they chatted away most of the afternoon. She wanted to hear everything about Italy and Switzerland. She had been to Rome, but never Switzerland. At some point, Tyler told the story of how the women in Pescara could not believe Serena owned a construction company. They went on and on about it. The men became angry as the women started talking amongst themselves about owning their own businesses.

Aunt Pia laughed and laughed and seriously looked at Tyler and said "You know she is a gem. You hold on to her. You are perfect for each other."

Tyler said "I couldn't agree more. And yes, I don't plan on letting go of her. I may need some of your help convincing her."

"You don't need my help," Aunt Pia answered. "That girl is hooked. Don't screw it up."

"There you go again," Charlie said. "Why can't you just say you are happy for them."

Aunt Pia gave Tyler that exasperated look. Tyler said, "I get it and I promise I won't screw it up."

As he was leaving, his phone buzzed. Maury gave him two bits of news: On Monday, a representative from the Department of the Interior would pay him a visit. He/She would investigate the grounds, the room, and interview him for approval to continue remodeling. Maury said it was very good news. The person doing the interviewing would be a high-ranking official in the Historical Preservation arm of the DOI. Also, the hearing had been scheduled for the last week in March, starting Monday morning at 9AM. Judge Hastings would preside.

Tyler thanked him for the news and said he was forwarding some information Aunt Pia had given him, and mentioned that she had said it would help our case.

CHAPTER THIRTY-EIGHT

On Thursday, Tyler spoke to the culinary class and this time, even though prepared food wasn't involved, he had an even bigger audience. They had to meet in the auditorium. Given his international status, he had become a big deal to the students. The question-and-answer session lasted almost two hours. They picked his brain clean.

At Millie's Friday evening, Tyler took his normal ribbing and it brought him back down to earth. The big joke was the silver necklace with the silver burro pendant Serena had bought for Billy. He was still mad at her, and she took a good amount of sarcasm from him; still, he was wearing it. They had a great time.

Bright and early Monday morning, Ms. Smith from the DOI arrived and Tyler set about giving his guided tour, yet again. After the tour and a walk around the grounds, he asked her to please have a cup of coffee, which she agreed to. They sat at his kitchen table and talked.

"First and foremost, Mr. Harrington," she began, "these organizations did not have the right to get a cease-and-desist order on your construction. If you wanted to fight it in court, the judge would have had to throw it out immediately. I am surprised it was allowed, to begin with. Most people do not understand historic preservation and how it relates to property owners. If your house was designated as an historic property, then they could file that order. Any property that is a landmark would fall under the auspices of the National Park Service first and foremost. Until you apply for landmark status, you can do whatever you want with your property.[1] However, you do understand the historical significance of that room. It is living history and there has been much interest in how you will proceed. Can I offer you some advice?"

"I do understand the significance of that room," Tyler acknowledged. Please, what are your thoughts?"

"You know that big tree stump?" The agent explained. "It's in the way of the room and it will eventually rot, which could cause additional damage to the room. If you were to remove that stump, a lot of dirt would be displaced. And, the wood ceiling is showing wear and tear with rotting and smaller roots coming through. You could dig the stump out, dig to the current roof line of the room, put a new roof over the old one to keep it as original as possible, and replace the dirt back onto the new roof, a little less I'd say, not to stress the old wood."

Tyler finished the thought. "Then, with the big hole, we can make an entrance way into the room, using a concrete ramp leading to that outer door. The house would not be needed as an entryway, and multiple visitors could enter at one time. We could hang pictures of the room as it is now, as a display, with the pictures of the gold and all."

"Exactly," Ms. Smith responded. You wouldn't need Landmark status for that, and if you accept funds from the DOI, we will maintain the room."

"That's where I think we may have an issue," Tyler countered. "There is no parking here, and there isn't enough land to make it a tourist destination. What I could do is give access to Academia and other interested groups and limit the visitation to, say, the first Saturday of every month for 8 hours, by reservation only, up to 200 people a day. It will keep curiosity at a high level, rather than somewhere to go and something to do. 10,400 visitors a year is no small number, at least in my book. And, we could accept private donations only, for upkeep and staffing the tours. We could purchase a bus, keep it in town for their use also, and bus visitors here, which would mean that we would not need parking. I know a bunch of people who would like to run a tour bus full time."

Ms. Smith answered, "I think you have it. Submit this plan in writing to me, along with architectural specifics and plans, so we can move forward. We'll inspect the job as it progresses and give a final ok when it is complete. This way, no organizations will get in your way. You will be officially, yet unofficially, under the auspices of the DOI. In the meantime, get some heat in here. No offense."

"None taken," Tyler answered. "And thank you very much. When this is made public, a lot of people will be happy."

That evening, over a glass of wine, Tyler described to Serena what Ms. Smith had suggested. He went over all of it. They discussed it at length, and she was on board. "I guess you'll need a great contractor?" She asked playfully.

Tyler answered, "Only if she is free from other obligations, has a great body, and a potty mouth."

CHAPTER THIRTY-NINE

Not all of the states were in alignment prior to the hearing date. The judge postponed the hearing until the second week of April.

Once the cease-and-desist order was lifted, and Serena had finished with most of the courthouse project, she made good on her word. She and most of her crew joined Charlie and his couple of guys, turning the house into a beehive of activity. His funds were holding out. Yet he knew the garage and workshop would have to be put on hold for a while. And, he had to prolong the employment of the architect for the outside entrance work. It, and the garage, needed to blend with the house to keep its historical look. That was very important to Tyler.

The old furnace in the basement was a bear to remove. Charlie cussed the whole time, as he tried to get it out. They basically took it apart and removed pieces that were still hard to get up the brand new cellar steps, which had been recently installed. The ductwork, as well as all needed wall removals were creating a lot of dust, which forced Tyler to spend a couple of nights at Serena's apartment. The upside was a warmer night's sleep.

While the ductwork was in progress, and all plumbing had been completed, the upstairs bathroom shower was installed, replacing the old tub with a new tub of similar design. It had been a bedroom once and there was plenty of room for the fixtures and a nice large vanity. Serena took over that project and made it to her liking. Tyler knew her eye was much better than his own, as to the diverse and future needs of a one-bathroom house. The commode and a small sink were installed in an area that had access to two doors; one going in from the bathroom and one coming from the hallway—More or less a powder room. That way, if the shower was in use, the commode would still be available. An additional commode was installed in the main bathroom. Tyler thought it was a great idea, given that the house had four bedrooms, and the possibility of a large family living in the house.

The furnace and AC were installed once the ductwork was finished. The old plaster walls had to be torn down due to the duct-work installation. New insulation and drywall was put up. All of the floors were sanded and stained, as well as all of the fireplaces and any other wood pieces, like the banister. All new light fixtures were installed to complement the era, with nothing neo-modern. The natural wood grains stood out immediately and were very attractive.

One weekend in late March, Kathy and Jerry came to visit with the kids. Tyler stayed with Serena because there were only two bedrooms in the house. Early the next morning, Serena and Kathy confiscated Tyler's credit card and they went furniture shopping. When they came back, Tyler just smiled when he saw all of the receipts. Serena was very shy about it, and did not know how Tyler would react after all of the money they had spent. She was so happy. Kathy said Serena had picked out most of the furniture and they even found a couple of great antique pieces for the downstairs hallway and great room. Tyler made sure she knew it was ok and he was glad they had a blast shopping. The kitchen was his baby and would wait until everything else was done. The house was shaping up to everything he had anticipated. Even the small water closet had been enlarged into a decent sized powder room.

Kathy and Jerry said their goodbyes on Sunday. They were planning to get a babysitter so they could be back for the hearing. And, they would all be able to stay at the house.

CHAPTER FORTY

The day of the hearing finally came. Serena came downstairs to find Tyler and Maury drinking coffee in the kitchen. Kathy and Jerry joined them a few minutes later.

Maury said "I slept like a baby last night—warm. The last time I stayed here, my nose froze solid."

Tyler told the story of the first night he and Serena had spent together on New Year's Eve. They all laughed at the story and were in a good mood. Kathy could not get over how nice the house looked with all of the furniture they had bought. Tyler complimented her and Serena for the wonderful job they had done making the house look like a home. Everyone got dressed and were soon out the door headed to the courthouse in town.

A media circus it was. Outside of the courtroom were TV vans and a slew of reporters not able to get into the courtroom. Tyler, Maury, and James Dobson were seated at a table on the left side of the courtroom. On the right, a large table held ten attorneys, two from each state represented in the lawsuit. Directly behind Tyler's table sat Serena, Kathy, Jerry, Charlie, and Sandra. Behind them was Barbara, Craig, Janice, Billy, and Debra, the editor of the paper. And behind them, were other friends and spectators. Behind the attorneys' table representing the five states were at least twenty additional attorneys and aides. The courtroom was completely filled.

The judge came in and opened the proceedings. After reading the complaints filed by each state, the judge, Nathan Henry, summarized the complaints and offered them as one and the same: each state is due the gold with their state emblem on them and without proof of ownership from the defendants, the remaining gold belonged to each state divided equally.

The Judge looked to Maury and he opened with "Your Honor, my clients accept the proof of ownership of the marked gold bars. That is not in question here. His contention is that the unmarked gold was hidden by his ancestor and is rightfully his."

The day went on as each state's attorney rose and gave testimony as to why the defendant had no concrete proof as to the ownership of the gold. They argued the gold could have been stolen by his ancestors and hidden there, having been not rightfully theirs originally. The conjecture by each was more far-fetched than the previous claim. At one point, they even argued amongst themselves regarding their claims, North Carolina stating it was found on their soil. It was evident there really wasn't a consensus among the states. There was written evidence from the state of Tennessee, from 1859, according to which a meeting's minutes of the state financial committee discussed an audit revealing missing gold from their treasury. It ended with certain members assigned to find the reason for the missing funds. No subsequent information was ever revealed in following meetings' minutes. It proved the gold came from Tennessee.

Tyler felt sickened by the proceedings. He had just gone through his breakup and betrayal over greed and lust. These people were acting like the gold was their own and would defend it to their deaths. The amount was a drop in the bucket, considering the budgets of most state legislatures. But they were tasked with bringing home whatever they could get, more than they had already been ceded to by the court. Each state would get over $3.6 million, with another $3.6 million at stake.

They broke for lunch. Tyler mentioned his apprehension and disgust to Serena, who listened objectively and reassured him everything would be ok. In the end, they would still have each other. Maury said everything was going just as they had discussed.

After lunch, it was Maury's turn to address the court. He turned it over to James Dobson, who introduced himself to the court and described his specialty. He started by quoting common law classifications of found treasure:

Lost Property — Where the owner has unintentionally misplaced his property.

Abandoned Property — Where the owner has discarded or voluntarily terminated ownership.

Treasure Trove — Where the owner has hidden gold, silver, bullion, or plate, or other items such as paper money.

Mislaid Property — Where the owner intentionally left property in a place where he can get to it.

Embedded property — Where the treasure has become part of the natural earth. [1]

James continued, "It is our contention that the gold is a treasure trove that has not been mislaid, abandoned, or lost. It was embedded behind a stone wall for safe keeping, and later access to. According to common law, the owner of the property has the right of possession. However, any treasure trove must be returned to its rightful owner if that owner can be identified, without a doubt." [2]

He paused and let that statement sink in.

Maury then took over and said, "Your honor, I would like to present our exhibit A to the court."

A large screen TV was rolled in and the video Serena had shot was played, while Maury narrated the events—

"I would like to show the court that they were both *not* aware of the hidden room and false wall behind which the gold bars were truly hidden."

"Your Honor, I would like to present our exhibit B," he went on.

The North Carolina Attorney jumped up and said "Your

Honor, we object to this exhibit and do not acknowledge the legitimacy of this testimony. This person is 95 years old and cannot possibly provide testimony for this hearing. This information is purely conjecture on the part of an elderly citizen."

The judge looked at Maury and said, "Mr. Greenbaum, do you have any information to qualify this testimony?"

"Your Honor," he began, "Mrs. Pia Henderson is 95 years old and has arthritis. She has a master's degree in History from the University of North Carolina, has published three books on the history of Eastern North Carolina during her tenure as an adjunct professor at Eastern Carolina University. She has been published in numerous magazine articles over the years and has written countless papers on a variety of historical subjects, mainly on the internet. I may also add she was heavily involved in the civil rights movement in North Carolina, and, on two occasions, walked with Dr. Martin Luther King Jr. She is still well respected nationally for her achievements and continues to be a resource on historical events. As a side note, she is proficient on a laptop and on the internet, and can still run circles around most of the people in this room." The last statement received a laugh from the crowd.

Judge Henry responded "Mr. Greenbaum, the court is well aware of the accomplishments of Mrs. Henderson. But, I'm not sure of the relevance. If she were here to explain it may have been better."

"Your honor," Maury started, "She is 95 and..."

Just then Barbara handed her phone to Tyler who handed the phone to Maury. Maury read a text.

"Mr. Greenbaum," the judge said.

"Your Honor, this is a text from Mrs. Henderson."

The judge said "Barbara Hastings, if I see that phone again, I will kick you out of this courtroom and hold you in contempt of court."

"Yessir," she replied.

"Your Honor," Maury went on, ignoring Barbara's rebuke,

"Mrs. Henderson says she regrets she wasn't able to attend today and testify. She says the courtroom does not have a witness box that has a ramp for her wheelchair. Otherwise, she would have attended."

Judge Henry hesitated, turned red, and called the bailiff over, while holding his hand over the microphone, and whispered something into his ear. He then gathered himself and said, "The court will allow the testimony."

The other attorneys all objected and, while the judge silenced the courtroom, Maury leaned over to Tyler and said "I have to meet that woman. She has bigger balls than I do. Just brilliant."

"Everyone has been given the packet in front of you prior to the hearing," Maury continued. Page 1 shows a map of the pyrite belt that runs from just south of Washington DC to central Virginia in a southwest direction. The accompanying information establishes the belt through the US Geological Survey.³

Page 2 provides the history of gold mining in Virginia, from placer mines in 1804 through lode mining up until the discovery of gold in California in 1849. Gold mining in Virginia ceased during the Civil War.⁴

Page 3 shows a map of the known gold mines in Spotsylvania County, Virginia. There were literally dozens of mines, mines that were recorded and deeded.⁵

Page 4 shows the record of a deed purchased by Virgil Thorne in 1840 for 10 acres of land along the Rapidan river in Spotsylvania, Virginia.

Page 5 shows a transfer of deed from Virgil Thorne to a Mr. John Wellford 5 months later. John Wellford was the owner of Catharine Furnace in Spotsylvania County. He and his partners had built the furnace in 1837 and produced pig iron."

An attorney jumped up and said, "Your Honor, how do we know these documents are accurate?"

Maury paused and went on after a few moments, "Your Honor, Mrs. Henderson was able to collect this information from her contacts throughout the Historical Societies that exist in this country. The Department of Interior manages Catharine Furnace and one of its bibliographers read about the gold found here and got curious. She pulled records from Spotsylvania Courthouse that go back to the mid-18th century. And Virgil Thorne was listed, Tyler's great grandfather, 2 times removed."

He once again paused to let the information sink in. Then he went for it—

"Your Honor, we conclude that Virgil Thorne struck it rich with gold mining, smelted the gold into bars at Catharine Furnace, and transferred and hid the gold in his house, the house built after his return to North Carolina."

Each opposing attorney jumped up in turn and objected. It was pandemonium for about five minutes. They wanted more proof. It was all conjecture; all lies, etc. Tyler felt sick to his stomach.

Judge Henry ordered a recess.

Maury, James, and Tyler went to a side room. Serena called to Maury and signaled if she could follow. Maury motioned to the Bailiff to let her by.

Maury and James went to the restroom and Serena sat on Tyler's lap. He was obviously distressed by the whole thing. She tried to comfort him and make him feel at ease. She sat in a chair when Maury and James came back.

Maury started. "Tyler, James and I chatted briefly in the restroom. What I told you a couple of months ago has come true, correct?

Tyler agreed. Serena interrupted and asked if she needed to leave.

Tyler said "Serena, whatever happens, you are a part of my life. Please stay. I need you."

She sat back down and Maury continued. "There is another solution you may not want to hear. In all court cases, there is always a chance for an agreed-upon settlement. It doesn't always have to be a win or lose. I am only throwing this up as an option. You found the gold. We all believe the unmarked gold belonged to your ances-tors. But they don't. They are already planning an appeal if things don't go their way. We could be in court for years. If you were to say, settle for 10% of all of the gold as a finder's fee and relinquish the rest, they may accept the terms and then, we just let them fight over ownership. You'll be out of any further litigation."

Tyler said "Maury, that may be the best idea I've heard all day."

Serena blurted "*Tyler.* Do you understand what that means?"

Tyler looked at Maury and said, "Will you and James approach the judge and let him know we are amicable to a settlement?"

Maury said "Are you sure? That is a lot of money you are leaving on the table. I don't want you to come back to me in our old age and accuse me of convincing you of this."

Tyler said "No. Give me a couple of minutes with Serena while you both talk to the judge."

Maury and James left the room. Tyler looked at Serena and said "I know what I want now and I want you. You are the best thing that ever happened to me. You are my found treasure. I love you. Will you marry me?"

Serena was stunned. She looked at him and said "Yes, I will marry you. Are you sure it's not the emotional turmoil you are going through?

"NO," he replied categorically. "Sitting here thinking about everything, the only sure thing I know is that I want to be with you, no matter what. When it hit me, I remembered what Aunt Pia said. She said 'Don't screw it up. Hang on to that girl.' I want to hang on to you for the rest of my life. Marry me!"

She jumped into his arms and started crying. Nothing was ever so clear to Tyler as were his feelings for her. Serena finally said "I have loved you since the day we met at the truck. I don't know how or why. But I fell hard for you, right then and there."

They gathered themselves, laughed, talked, and twenty minutes later, the lawyers were back.

Maury said, "We talked to the judge and he called the other

attorney's into his chambers. We negotiated and what came up was a counteroffer of 5%."

Tyler said "Here's what we are going to do. Serena, please make sure everyone out there stays when this is over."

She smiled, kissed him, and left the room, walking in a cloud.

CHAPTER FORTY-ONE

The Judge reconvened thirty minutes later than they should have. Everyone in the audience was wondering what was going on and were getting fidgety.

Judge Henry announced to the court that a settlement agreement had been reached and he would now read the agreement for the record.

"Tyler Harrington, as the owner of the property and finder of the treasure, has given up all claim to the gold."

Charlie said loudly, "Tyler, no!"

Judge Henry banged his gavel and said "Charlie Washington, one more word and I'll throw you out. And that goes for anyone else who creates a disturbance during these proceedings."

"Tyler Harrington, as the owner of the property and finder of the treasure, has given up all claim to the gold. He has settled for a finder's fee of 5% of the total amount of all the gold. He relinquishes all further claims to the treasure and has asked and has been granted tax-free status from the state of North Carolina, in lieu of the return North Carolina will receive from his relinquishing claims on the gold. The state has accepted that status."

He finished "The remaining gold is in dispute by the five states present and will be litigated at another time. Mr. Harrington, I understand there is a lot of money involved here. However, I applaud your decision and wish you the best of luck with further endeavors."

The crowd was stunned. All of Tyler's friends just sat there speechless. The other people in the audience left after the judge retired and Tyler's group sat there waiting, as Serena had asked, as Tyler and Maury finished up the particulars with the court reporter. Tyler asked Maury and James to join him with his friends.

As they approached the group, the judge walked by, looked at Charlie, and said "You tell Pia I have a bone to pick with her."

Charlie said 'ok,' laughing. He looked at Maury and James and said "She got him elected District Attorney years ago with her endorsement. That man loves her."

Tyler approached the group, grabbed Serena, and Charlie said "I cannot believe you gave that money away. I cannot believe it." Sandra nudged him.

Barbara chimed in "Seriously, Tyler. Please explain."

Tyler said "Maury." Maury pulled out a piece of paper and read "As you heard from the judge, the finder's fee was settled at 5% of approximately $37 million dollars. Tyler has all too generously given James and me 10% as our fee. I admonished him for that, but he won't take no for an answer."

Tyler added "It's a retainer, Maury, for future issues. I don't think the Department of the Interior is done with me yet."

Maury continued, "After our fee, the remainder is tax free from the state, but not the Federal Government. The rate is somewhere around 40% of treasure as taxable income. The remainder, after taxes which will be paid up front, comes to approximately 1 million dollars. Half of that money will be given to Charlie and Sandra Washington to disperse with their family as they see fit."

Charlie jumped up again and said "Tyler, you *are* crazy."

Tyler said "Charlie, the Washington family was part of the whole gold caper. Zachariah Washington was hanged for it. He knew where that gold was, which is why he didn't talk. He was protecting both families since Virgil Thorne was dead. Sarah and

Phoebe grew old together, best friends who had a shared history. They took some gold with them and lived out the rest of their lives knowing there was more. But they didn't go after it, leaving well enough alone."

For once Charlie was speechless.

Tyler said "I wanted you all to stay to hear this. Six Months ago, I was beyond despair. I lost my parents in a car crash, which left me alone, a girlfriend that cheated on me and stole my restaurant right out from under me. I was completely alone in this world. I bought that house on a whim and for therapy."

"Then I met Serena and fell in love, real love as I had always imagined. And with her came all of you, real friends, true friends who I now consider my family, and who all hopefully feel the same about me."

They all started talking at once. Tyler held up his hand and they got quiet.

"All of you think I lost a treasure today. I am here in front of you to tell you that all of you" pointing at them, "are the treasure I found. Without you, I couldn't have gone through this alone. And lastly," grabbing Serena by the shoulders and hugging her, "this lady has agreed to marry me, the real treasure."

Barbara screamed and jumped up and down. All of the women rushed forward and hugged Serena.

Debra, the editor, leaned over to Billy and said, "I thought she was a lesbian?"

Billy said, "Long story; not a story you want to print."

Debra said "This gold hearing is good enough for now. And from what I just heard, there is more to the story."

CHAPTER FORTY-TWO

That evening, at Tyler's house, they all sat around drinking wine and Single Malt Scotch Charlie had brought. Maury had left for home with pending business. James Dobson had left for Raleigh. Janice and Billy had left, but not before Janice made Serena promise not to get married before she and Billy did. Barbara and Craig also had to get home to the kids.

Charlie kept going over and over how he wouldn't know what to do with that much money. Tyler and Serena talked about the plans they had for the room under the house. So, Charlie thought about starting a tram business in town for tours and the like. And, he and Sandra had good ideas on how to disperse some of the money to the living heirs of the Washington Clan, to be put to good use.

"I have got to meet Aunt Pia," Kathy said. "She sounds as though she is the type of woman I would like to become." Serena made arrangements with Sandra for them to be there in the morning before the stories began.

The next morning, the guys went off to the hardware store early. Kathy was already drinking coffee when Serena came down. She looked at Serena and said "What's wrong?"

Serena said "I don't know. I just don't feel well. I'm not sure if it's all of the excitement or the wine I had last night. I'll bathe and shake it off."

They went into Aunt Pia's house and Sandra had her dressed nicely for visitors. She looked at Kathy and said "Now, aren't you a sight. Tyler has good taste in women, doesn't he?"

Kathy said "Oh, I can tell you some stories about that guy. But Serena wouldn't appreciate them."

Aunt Pia cackled and said "All men are alike. You just have to know how to handle them."

Serena bent down and gave her a kiss. Aunt Pia congratulated her and told her had finally found the right man. She grabbed her face and, as she was lifting it up, she said "What's wrong with you?"

"Nothing. I just feel a little off today," Serena answered.

"When you had your issues and spent hours here watching the stories with me, I got to know you pretty well," Aunt Pia insisted. "I know something is up."

Serena said "Well, I think all of the excitement has overwhelmed me. I'm just feeling a little sick today."

Aunt Pia looked into her face for a good thirty seconds and said, "Girl, you are with child! Sandra, look at that face. It's shining and round. I know a pregnant girl when I see one."

Kathy jumped up all excited and looked at Serena, looked at Aunt Pia, looked at Sandra, and said "How do you know?"

"When you have been around as many young women as I have, you just know," Aunt Pia said. "Plus, Charlie said those two have been like rabbits in a hutch. It makes sense."

They spent another two hours there until the stories came on and left. First stop was the drug store. They got home and sure enough, Aunt Pia was right.

Tyler was ecstatic. Kathy thought he was going to cry. He looked at Serena and said, "We are going to fill this house up."

Serena said "Whoa. Simmer down, big guy. One at a time."

Of course, she spent the next two hours talking to Barbara and Janice.

CHAPTER FORTY-THREE

The next couple of weeks went by quickly until the excitement, newspaper columns, and well-wishers started to die down. Tyler and Serena worked into a routine with Serena going to work and Tyler finishing up the 1001 little jobs that go with a remodel. It was a good time. And they also spent some time metal detecting in the woods, still on their property.

One day, they went down into the room and looked at the big root, with the small roots coming through the boards in the ceiling. They looked at the integrity of the cots, table, and bookcase. Someone eventually would try to sit on a cot and it would just disintegrate. They would have to replace the blankets and pillows because they were too far gone. Once again, Tyler made a list for them to consider. On the way to the ladder, Serena bent down and picked up a button. It was a little metal button, probably brass.

She said, "You know, Tyler, there may be some items scattered around here. We should bring the metal detector down here and check.

"Why not," he said; and went up the ladder to get the equipment. He was back down in minutes and started the grid at the far end of the room by the cots. Serena took the pinpoint detector and started scanning the corners around the floor. As Tyler moved across on his first pass, Serena was under the big root bent over, searching the corner. Tyler moved the long-handled detector with the square head right up to her protruding rear end, and he couldn't resist; he turned it up sideways and goosed her. She jumped up immediately from the shock and held the pinpoint detector like a knife above her head as though she was going to stab him. She was laughing when the detector started going crazy. They both stopped and looked at each other. She turned and started scanning around the wall and, when she came to the root, it went off again. She went around and under the root towards dirt, and the detector screamed once again. There was some heavy metal behind the root.

They stood back for a minute, she punched him for goosing her, and both stared at the root. They decided to cut the root near the wall to get it entirely out of the way. Tyler had a hand saw and a hatchet. They didn't know which one would work.

The root was old but still thick. It took almost an hour to cut it through, along with all of its side branches. They put the pinpoint detector back into the dirt and still had to cut another two or three branches out. They had been at it for almost an hour and a half. With one smaller root gone, Serena put the pinpoint detector into the dirt and they heard a clang, like it was hitting a dish. The floor under them was covered with branches, dirt, and saw dust, but they managed to scoop the remaining dirt out anyway. They saw a pottery jar, more of a crock, with a wide mouth, covered and sealed with wax. It looked like a Sauerkraut crock. They finally pried it loose, careful not to break it, and held it in the light. It was about the size of a football and similar in shape, although the bottom was flat and the oval top was larger and flat and covered with a wax seal, which completely covered the lid. Tyler reached back into the hole in the earth and searched around with the pinpoint detector, but it didn't go off again.

They took the jar upstairs and inspected it on the kitchen table. After a brief discussion, they assumed the crock had been buried many years ago and had been consumed by the roots of the tree as the tree kept growing. How else could it have gotten tangled in the roots like that?

Tyler used a kitchen knife to cut around the base of the lid where the wax was thickest. It mostly crumbled as he put pressure on it. The wax gave way and he started to remove the lid, which was made of wood. Under the wood were fibers that looked like coconut hair, crammed into the top of the jar. As they pulled the fibers out, they saw cloth bundles underneath. Tyler grabbed the first bundle and handed it to Serena. She carefully unwrapped the bundle and examined it, saying "This is oilcloth. It was used to protect things from moisture." The opening showed a small pouch. She took one of the cloth napkins from a drawer and emptied the pouch on the napkin. Out fell a dozen diamonds that were at least 5 carats each. Tyler handed her another bundle, about the same size as the first one. She poured it and out came six rubies and four emeralds, the likes of which they had never seen. They were large, at least 10 carats each, and beautifully cut. The third bundle had five sapphires that were beautifully cut and looked like the rubies and emeralds, as though they all belonged together as a set. The last small bundle held gold coins stamped with images they had never seen.

They looked at each other speechless. At the very bottom was an oil cloth around a small wooden box. The box was wax sealed; Tyler carefully pried the wax off, which was surprisingly still firm compared to the outer wax seal. Inside the box was another oilcloth, that once removed, showed a necklace. Tyler and Serena were stunned, literally speechless. Serena held up the necklace. The silver chain had barely tarnished. The entire chain was lined with 1-carat diamonds in silver settings. In the middle at the neck was at least a 5-carat emerald cut diamond set into the chain. There were two more chain loops, one beginning three fourths of the way around the main necklace on each side, and the other beginning just inside that loop. The loop at the bottom contained twenty 1-carat diamonds with a 5-carat emerald cut diamond in the middle. The middle loop contained five diamonds on each side, all 3 carats or more, with what looked like a 20-carat oval cut blue diamond as the entire centerpiece.

They were both shaking. Tyler said, "Take your t-shirt off." Still in shock, she said, "OK."

The necklace was so large, he told her, "Lower your bra so this hits only skin."

She just took her bra off as he latched the necklace in place from behind, pushing her hair aside. When he came back around to the front, he stared for a good minute.

Then he said, "Have you ever had booty wearing pirate booty?"

"No," she answered. "Have I ever told you I love the way you think?"

They were careful not to disturb any of the gems. Afterwards, as they were sipping a glass of wine, Tyler said "What are the odds of finding two treasure troves in the same house? They have to be astronomical."

The only logical explanation had to be Teach or Bonnet. Someone who knew these waters knew of this knoll and the young oak. However, they never raided in the Indian Ocean as far as anyone had written. These gems did not come from the Caribbean unless Avery traded them while he was there. These have to be from his big heist in the Gulf of Aden. How, and why they ended up here is purely conjecture and speculation.

Tyler repeated himself. "What are the odds of finding two treasure troves in the same house?"

"Like a needle in a stack of needles," Serena answered.

"And you made fun of me," Tyler stated.

After a couple more sips, she said "Now what? Do we call the sheriff?"

Tyler thought for a minute and said "Serena, you are my treasure. These are just trinkets in life that have little meaning. I will treasure you always."

She laid a big kiss on him. "I love that you feel that way. And I feel whole-heartedly the same about you. We still have to do something with these gems. Do we call the sheriff?"

Tyler said "No, we don't call the sheriff just yet. We'll document everything we just found, since you demanded to video that damn root as we cut. That way we have proof of the find. We'll put everything in a safety deposit box for now. We'll only give the necklace and the gold coins to the sheriff."

"Tyler, why only the necklace and coins?"

"The necklace is a work of art; more than just a valuable item. It will create quite the stir. The gold coins are historical and should be given to whomever can properly display them. We'll keep the other gems, which are much less conspicuous. You'll need a wedding ring, right?"

"Tyler, you can't be serious?"

"Yes, I am," he said.

Over the last several weeks, he had been reviewing events and results. Why were the state's attorneys so adamant about retrieving the gold? What could they possibly gain in the long run by taking all of the gold rather than half of it? Were they doing their jobs or was there more to it? Was it greed? Or was it something else? What was owed? And to whom?

The pirates had attacked and took property from merchants and people on the high seas. They sometimes killed the defenders of the ship. That was just plain greed.

His ancestors found gold and had to hide it due to its sheer amount and the political circumstances. He believed, as farmers, Virgil and Zack had hit it rich and went to extreme lengths to hide their findings. That gold eventually killed Zack. Phoebe and Sarah wanted nothing more to do with the gold because of what had happened. They gave it up to keep their families intact. Tyler thought they were two of the smartest and bravest people he could ever want to emulate.

He had enough money now to finish his house and move on. Maybe a teaching job at the high school? International travel with the team? Marry Serena, have kids, and live a life free from vast riches and the threat of constantly having to safeguard it?

Now, a necklace that would likely be considered priceless, along with gold coins from a different age —Who would come out of the woodwork and claim these items? He had no clue. These thoughts raced through his mind, as he kept looking at Serena with the necklace on. All he knew was he wanted her more than anything else.

The thought finally came to him to make a big splash with these finds. The necklace and coins were gone in his mind. Someone would want them, someone would claim them, and someone would fight for them. Just plain greed. He wanted no part of it. The gems, on the other hand, were much smaller and would not create a splash. If he held on to the gems, no one would think anything of it, if he were to sell them in the future.

Tyler said off-handedly "Take my property once, shame on you. Take my property twice, shame on me. The gems will be the future for our children. We'll keep them in a safety deposit box and if we ever need them, they will be there. If we never sell them, so be it."

Serena said, "Did I ever tell you I love the way you think!?"

The End

TIMELINES

Treasure Found
Timelines

Eb 1788-1861
 Virgil 1818-1865Zack 1819-1866
 Tyler 1843-1928Zack Jr 1852-1935
 Tyler Jr 1878-1964Zack III 1889-1974
 Henry H. 1928-1998John 1925-2009
 Married Sarah Thorne,
 (daughter of Tyler Jr.)
 George H. 1958-2019Charlie 1960-2021 Living
 Tyler 1988-2021 LivingAuntie Pia 1926-2021 Living

ACKNOWLEDGMENTS

I would like to thank my wife Michelle for her support and storyline advice, as well as John and Tina for their advice and recommendations. Will Atkinson for his inspiration and advice and Sharnette for her help.

And, my talented granddaughter Hadleigh for the artwork.

Thank you Stacey Smekofske for your help in publishing.

NOTES

PREFACE

1. "Treasure." Merriam-Webster.com Dictionary, Merriam-Webster, https://www.merriam-webster.com/dictionary/treasure. Accessed 6 Dec. 2021.

CHAPTER 1

1. W. J. Wallace, "Review: Knights of the Golden Circle," *Journal of Southern Religion* 15 (2013): http://jsr.fsu.edu/issues/vol15/wallace.html
David C. Keehn. *Knights of The Golden Circle: Secret Empire, Southern Secession, Civil War.* Baton Rouge: Louisiana State University Press, 2013. [ISBN 978-0-80715-004-7]

CHAPTER 2

1. blackpast.org/african-american-history/cheyney-university-pennsylvania-1837/

CHAPTER 3

1. https://en.wikipedia.org/wiki/Catharine_Furnace

CHAPTER 6

1. https://www.history.com/topics/american-civil-war/shermans-march
2. American Heritage Publishing, *American Heritage Picture History of the Civil War and Bruce Catton*, (Bonanza Books 1960) Pages 417-418

CHAPTER 11

1. https://en.wikipedia.org/wiki/Edenton,_North_Carolina#:~:text=Edenton%20was%20established%20in%201712,who%20had%20died%20that%20year.

CHAPTER 14

1. https://ncsweetpotatoes.com/sweet-potato-industry/

CHAPTER 22

1. Eric Jay Dolin. *Black Flags, Blue Waters: The Epic History of America's Most Notorious Pirates.* Liveright Publishing, 2019. [ISBN-13:9781631496226]
2. Eric Jay Dolin. *Black Flags, Blue Waters: The Epic History of America's Most Notorious Pirates.* Liveright Publishing, 2019. [ISBN-13:9781631496226]
3. Eric Jay Dolin. *Black Flags, Blue Waters: The Epic History of America's Most Notorious Pirates.* Liveright Publishing, 2019. [ISBN-13:9781631496226]
4. Eric Jay Dolin. *Black Flags, Blue Waters: The Epic History of America's Most Notorious Pirates.* Liveright Publishing, 2019. [ISBN-13:9781631496226]
5. https://www.gemsociety.org/article/the-history-of-lapidary/#Where_did_gem_-cutting_get_its_start?
6. https://www.gemsociety.org/article/the-history-of-lapidary/#Where_did_gem_-cutting_get_its_start?
7. Eric Jay Dolin. *Black Flags, Blue Waters: The Epic History of America's Most Notorious Pirates.* Liveright Publishing, 2019. [ISBN-13:9781631496226]
8. Eric Jay Dolin. *Black Flags, Blue Waters: The Epic History of America's Most Notorious Pirates.* Liveright Publishing, 2019. [ISBN-13:9781631496226]
9. Eric Jay Dolin. *Black Flags, Blue Waters: The Epic History of America's Most Notorious Pirates.* Liveright Publishing, 2019. [ISBN-13:9781631496226]

CHAPTER 36

1. *Buried Treasure Finders Keepers & the Law.* Cecil C. Kuhne II

CHAPTER 38

1. https://www.nps.gov/subjects/historicpreservation/laws.htm

CHAPTER 40

1. *Buried Treasure Finders Keepers & the Law.* Cecil C. Kuhne III
2. *Buried Treasure Finders Keepers & the Law.* Cecil C. Kuhne III
3. U.S. Department of the Interior | U.S. Geological Survey https://pubs.usgs.gov/sir/2006/5085/index.html
   Page Contact Information: Publishing Services Page Last Modified: 19:08:53 Thu 01 Dec 2016
4. Sweet, P.C. (1971): "Gold mines and prospects in Virginia: Virginia Minerals" *Virginia Division of Mineral Resources* Vol. 17, pp. 25-35.

5. Sweet, P.C. (1971): "Gold mines and prospects in Virginia: Virginia Minerals" Vol. 17, *Virginia Division of Mineral Resources*, pp. 25-35.

Made in the USA
Middletown, DE
16 September 2022

10640971R00124